# River Rest

# River Rest

by Susan Page Davis

Published in association with Tea Tin Press
ISBN **978-0-9972308-3-3**
Cover image by Lisa Bryant
Cover design by Roseanna White

*"Come unto me, all ye that labor and are heavy laden, and I will give you rest. Take my yoke upon you, and learn of me; for I am meek and lowly in heart, and ye shall find rest unto your souls, for my yoke is easy, and my burden is light." Matthew 11:28-30, KJV*

# Chapter 1

*September, 1918*
*Sidney, Maine*

Muffled hoofbeats drew Judith to the kitchen window over the cast iron sink. A smart buggy, drawn by a plump bay horse, rolled into the Chadbournes' driveway.

Judith yanked her apron off, ignoring her racing pulse. She barely knew Ben Thayer, the gentleman farmer up the road, and she wasn't sure she wanted to greet him today—especially given his errand.

She hurried to her father's room and tapped on the door panel. He didn't answer, so she opened the door, hoping he was awake. Since her mother's death six weeks ago, he had drawn deep into himself, neglecting the farm chores and hardly noticing what went on around him. Now he sat on the edge of the bed, his graying hair uncombed. Apparently he hadn't heard her knock.

"Pa," Judith said from the doorway. The bedclothes lay in a heap behind him, and his shirt was buttoned wrong, leaving the collar to flop at an odd angle. She spoke again, louder. "Ben Thayer's here, Pa."

He looked up and shoved something behind him.

"What is that?" She hurried across the room.

His shoulders drooped and he brought out the object he'd held. He glanced down at it then held it out with a resigned sigh.

Judith stared in horror at the revolver. He kept it for shooting varmints.

"Pa? What—"

Rapping at the front door interrupted her.

"Give me that!" She took the gun from his hand. Staring down at him, she tried to steady her breath. "That's Ben Thayer at the door, come to get Joel. You should go and speak to him."

Pa made no move to rise, but looked toward the window. Judith hurried out to the entry. Another knock came just before she reached the door and threw it open.

Thayer stepped back quickly, his eyes flaring. "Oh, Miss Chadbourne. I'm sorry. I thought no one had heard. Is Joel ready?"

"I'll call him."

Thayer's gaze had landed on the revolver in her hand, and his eyebrows shot up. "Oh." He peered at her uncertainly.

"It's. . .kind of you to take Joel with you." Judith tried to hide the gun in the folds of her skirt.

"Well, we both have to go, or Uncle Sam will say something about it." His eyebrows drew together. "Is everything all right?"

Judith looked up into his face. He was practically a stranger—she'd lived away from home, teaching school, most of the two years he'd been a neighbor. She had no desire to confide in him, and yet she owed him an explanation after answering the door with a gun in her hand. She attempted a smile, but failed miserably. A sob slipped out as she caught her breath.

He reached toward her but stopped short of touching her. "Is there anything I can do?"

She gulped and blinked past the tears filling her eyes. "Oh, Mr. Thayer, it's. . .it's Pa."

"Here. Let me take that." His fingers were as warm and gentle as his voice as he eased the revolver out of her grip. "Now, come sit down."

She turned toward the front room without the will to resist. When she stood in front of the sofa, the oddness of being here in the parlor with a man she barely knew hit her. She could handle a classroom full of children, or deal with people who came to buy butter or beans, but the mysterious artist who had bought the farm next door threw her into confusion.

"Joel is waiting for you out back with the children. Let me call him. The two of you need to go."

Thayer shook his head. "There's no hurry. The registrar will be there until the post office closes. Please, Miss Chadbourne. I don't mean to pry, but if there's any way I can help you. . ."

He scared her a little, with his short, crisp brown hair and intense blue eyes. She wasn't used to being so close to men, other than her father. But Ben Thayer had the reputation of being a nice man. A loner. A man who puttered about his farm, raising a few cattle because he wanted to, not because he needed money. An artist who painted on his walls. Mother had liked him. She'd said he was smarter than Professor Montgomery and Dr. Stearns combined. And Joel had told her that he kept a shiny, black Oldsmobile in his barn, under a sheet of canvas. No one could get much gasoline since the war started, so Thayer rarely took out the automobile, but relied on his horse like the other farmers—but he owned one. That in itself set him apart from most of her neighbors.

"I. . .he. . ."

"I only want to help, Miss Chadbourne. And it seems you might need some of that today."

She pulled in another shaky breath and squared her shoulders. "Ever since Mother died, Pa has seemed not to care if he lives or dies. He's let his beard grow, and he wears the same clothes day after day until I insist he change. Sometimes he sits for hours in his rocking chair, staring at the wallpaper."

"And this?" Ben held up the handgun with the muzzle pointed safely toward the floor.

She looked up into his pensive blue eyes. Inside her, the built-in wall of reserve cracked. "I went to his room just now, and he was holding it. Just sitting there, holding it. I'm afraid, Mr. Thayer." She sobbed and turned away. Shame washed over her for telling such a thing to someone outside the family.

After a long moment, he said softly, "And does your father have any more guns?"

Her heart leaped into her throat and she swung around. "Y-yes. He has a .22 and a deer rifle."

Thayer nodded, as though he'd expected that. "And where does he keep them?"

"In the closet under the stairs."

He looked down at the revolver. "If it would make you feel easier, I could take them to my house for safekeeping."

She flicked a glance at his face and read sympathy and concern. But should she trust him on such scant acquaintance? Perhaps she should tell Joel and let him hide his father's guns. But if they were somewhere in the house or barn, Pa might find them at another moment of deep depression. Better to have them off the premises.

"All right. Thank you." She cleared her throat. "I'll go for Joel. If you'll come this way, I'll show you the closet."

"Good. I'll take them to my buggy while you fetch your brother. And when you feel it's safe, I'll bring them back."

She left him in the hall to explore the closet and find the guns himself. She wouldn't have to tell Joel about their father's action if Mr. Thayer took them away, and Joel had enough to worry about already. A great weight lifted from her chest.

Passing Pa's door quietly, she went out the back door and along the ell to the barn. She found Joel and the children playing tag in the field next to the garden. It seemed a childish game for nineteen-year-old Joel, but he was about to leave childhood behind.

She wrapped her arms around herself. Tears burned in her eyes as Joel laughed and chased his younger siblings. Eight-year-old Ned, and Lydia, who was eleven, shrieked with glee. Bobby played, too, but Joel deliberately let the youngest escape him. Pain struck through her. Joel wasn't old enough to go to war. She wished she'd told Mr. Thayer not to mention the guns to Joel on their trip to town. Would he know that without her saying anything?

How old was Thayer, anyway? His offer to take Joel to the post office to register for the draft had surprised her. From what others had told her when he moved to the neighborhood, she'd thought he might be in his forties. Since coming home, she'd seen him several times from a distance at church services, and she'd revised that figure downward without curiosity. Now she wondered.

His contagious smile on pleasanter occasions made him look quite young, but he was older than thirty, Judith knew, because he was going to register today. Until this summer, only men from the ages of twenty-one to thirty had to register. Mr. Thayer was certainly older than twenty-one, Judith's age. And so he must also be more than thirty, or he would have registered before.

The battlefields in Europe seemed insatiable, and the age for conscription had recently been expanded. In the golden days of September, 1918, all those from eighteen to forty-five had to sign up.

Lydia caught sight of her and stopped running so abruptly that Joel caromed into her. She stumbled, and Joel reached out to steady her.

"You all right?"

"Yes," Lydia said.

Joel grinned. "You're it."

"Mr. Thayer's here," Judith called, and Joel looked her way. He stood still for a moment then walked toward her, combing his fingers through his hair.

When he reached her side, he looked back at the three younger children.

"'Bye, kids. See ya later."

He followed Judith inside, and the youngsters trailed after them. Sixteen-year-old Christina appeared on the stairway and hurried down to join them.

"Are you leaving?" she asked Joel.

"Yes, but I'll be back."

"What if they tell you to go to the army camp?" Ned asked.

"Then I'll go. But don't worry. I won't be called up today. They're just getting my name and address and that sort of thing." Joel's shoulders squared as he reached the front door.

Mr. Thayer waited on the front porch. He threw a meaningful look at Judith and nodded before greeting her brother. "Hello, Joel. All set?"

"I guess so." Joel glanced at Judith. "Should I tell Pa?"

"He knows," she said.

Joel nodded soberly.

"We should be back in an hour or so." Ben smiled at all the children. "Unless the lines are long, that is."

"Who will print the electric bills if you have to go to war?" Ned asked him soberly.

Ben raised his eyebrows. "That's a good question, Ned. Perhaps I should teach someone else to run my press just in case."

Judith was able to smile at that. One of Thayer's avocations was printing, and he'd lately begun to provide butter paper for farmers and letterheads for local businesses. Ned probably itched to see how the small press in the neighbor's dining room worked.

Thayer glanced at Joel. "Got your birth certificate?"

"Yes, sir." Joel patted his shirt pocket.

"Thank you, Mr. Thayer." Judith almost choked on the words. Would he think less of them now, knowing her father's dark secret? Judith and Joel had worked hard to keep up with the farm work and hide Pa's condition from other people, but their father only got worse. If he continued acting strangely, it was bound to come out, one way or another.

Joel was down the steps before she'd said a proper goodbye. She felt she ought to kiss him. But that was silly. They weren't off for the front lines. As Mr. Thayer had said, they would soon be back, and nothing would be changed. Except that their names would be on a list of able-bodied men available to go and fight. She shuddered.

Joel climbed into the buggy, and Ben took the driver's seat. The children watched as they drove away. The sleek horse trotted out the driveway, and the buggy soon disappeared around the bend in the road.

"Christina, you and Lydia help me get supper, won't you?" Judith turned to go back inside.

"Sure," said Christina.

Lydia frowned but followed her sisters to the kitchen without complaint. Ned and Bobby dashed toward the barn, no doubt hoping to escape being assigned chores. Judith let the younger girls pass her and paused before the hall closet. She could hear Christina talking to Lydia in the kitchen as they put on their aprons.

She opened the closet door. The two rifles were gone. So was the row of ammunition boxes that had stood on the shelf. She shut the door without a sound and went to the kitchen.

# Chapter 2

Judith opened the mailbox with nothing more on her mind than what she would cook for supper. One envelope sat in the cavernous box, looking a bit lonely. She took it out and gazed down at the return address, her stomach plunging.

Less than three weeks had passed since Joel had gone with Ben Thayer to register, but already he was receiving word from the federal government. She could only think of one reason for that.

She took the letter inside. Joel was in the kitchen, scalding the milk pail. She held out the envelope without speaking. He looked at her, seized a dish towel, and wiped his hands. Judith watched him get out his pocketknife and slit the envelope, wishing he would hurry but at the same time not wanted to know what was inside.

"I've been called up." Joel tore his gaze from the letter and looked bleakly into Judith's eyes. "So soon. I didn't really expect it. I'll go Monday."

"I knew it." Judith regretted the words as soon as they were out. She forced a smile. "So. I'll fix something special for tonight. Pies, maybe. You'll have to tell Pa."

"Think pies will help?"

Tears flooded her eyes. "Oh, Joel."

He folded her into his arms. "Shh. I'll be all right, Sis. But what about you?"

Judith gave him a squeeze and stepped back. She swiped a tear from her cheek with her sleeve. "We'll get by. But I was hoping ... Ben Thayer said we were near peace terms. I guess it wasn't very realistic to think you wouldn't have to go."

"We all hope it'll be over soon. But even when it's done, there will be work to do over there. They'll need fresh troops."

"Yes. I hope all the men get to come home soon."

Joel chucked her gently under the chin with his fist. "Cheer up. I think I'll step over to Ben's and tell him. I'll expect to smell pie cooking when I come back."

Judith's laugh turned into a sob. Concern returned to Joel's face, but she waved him away. "Go on. I won't say anything to Pa. You can tell everyone at supper." Their father might be less likely to rant in front of the children, but she doubted it.

"Right." Joel backed out the door with a crooked smile and hurried off.

Judith inhaled deeply and opened a drawer for her paring knife.

*****

On Saturday morning, Judith set bread dough to rise and covered the bowl with a clean linen dish towel. She drained the dry beans she'd soaked overnight and got out the bean pot.

"Got any coffee?" Joel burst through the back door with a tall, dark-haired young man on his heels.

"Harry! I heard you were home for the weekend." Judith set the bean pot on the counter and gave Joel's best friend a quick hug. "It's so good to see you."

"Thanks," Harry said.

"And yes, I have coffee."

"Great." Joel went to the cupboard for two mugs, and Judith began pouring the swollen beans into the brown-and-tan pot.

Harry was an agile, spirited boy of eighteen. A year younger than Joel, he had graduated from high school in the spring. He was always in the middle of the action in the neighborhood, whether it was a barn raising or a baseball game.

"How is everything at the camp?" Judith asked. "Do they feed you well?"

"Aw, it's all right. All the cooking's done by fellows, and it's not like home. But the rooms are pretty comfortable. It's a girls' school, you know."

"Yes, I heard." The army had taken over a private school in Lewiston, about fifty miles away, as its processing and training camp for Maine boys.

"I'm in a big room with eight other boys. We've got cots." She nodded.

"Harry says they expect to go to France," Joel said almost eagerly as he poured the coffee.

"It's not official," Harry said. "Couldn't tell you if it was. But that's what we all think. It should be soon now."

Judith nodded. A chance to go to France and do something for the cause of freedom was just the type of adventure Harry would relish. Would Joel be trained in time to go with his best friend's unit?

"We're going to take the train together on Monday," Joel said, and her stomach plummeted.

"Oh?"

"I'm glad it worked out this way, and I came home this weekend," Harry said.

"Yes. I'm glad you'll have a little time together at least." Judith didn't dare think beyond getting Joel to the training camp. Her family would be like the Gardners now, waiting for any scrap of news from the boy who had joined the army. But she couldn't say anything about her fear, or how much she hated all of this. Not with Harry and Joel putting such a brave face on it.

"How's your pa?" Harry asked. His face went so sober, Judith was sure Joel had confided in him, at least some of their worries.

"He's about the same."

Harry nodded.

Judith forced a smile. "We'll be picking the apples soon. I'm hoping he'll help us sort them and take them to the depot."

"He'd better," Joel said darkly. He set the coffeepot down on the back of the wood range and handed his friend a mug. "Come on, Harry. Let's go into the front room. Judith doesn't like anyone to get in her way when she's cooking."

"Have some cookies," she said.

Joel was already taking the cover off the cookie jar. Judith took a small plate from the cupboard and handed it to him. Joel frowned as if that was an unnecessary nicety, but he set down his mug and put half a dozen cookies on the plate. A moment later, the boys were gone. She could hear Harry's laugh from the front room, and Christina's high-pitched voice.

"Well, look who's here! Harry Gardner!"

"Hey, Christina! How are you doing?"

"I'm great, soldier boy. How are you?"

Judith stood still, listening for the answer. Harry had come wearing his old overalls and a worn work shirt, not his uniform. Why did Christina have to remind him that he was going back to the military camp in two days?

But Harry didn't seem to miss a beat. "I'm great! And you don't look so bad yourself."

"Thanks! Oh, yum, molasses cookies!"

Judith shut out the young voices and went back to work. Christina should be in here helping her, but who knew when her sister would have a chance to sit and talk to Joel again. Of course, she probably wouldn't bother if Harry hadn't come to call. Christina had kept an eye on Harry for at least a year before he enlisted. On her visits home from her teaching job, Judith had spoken to Mother about it.

"Harry's a good boy," Mother had said. "And a little flirtation never hurt a girl Christina's age."

Judith wondered about that. Mother hadn't seemed at all worried, but was she right? Something stubborn in the back of Judith's mind said that flirtations *could* hurt. She'd never indulged in them at sixteen. But then, she took everything more seriously than Christina did, and she didn't have Christina's dark, curly hair.

She sighed and reached for the molasses. Now that Mother was gone, it was her duty to keep Christina in line, not to mention the three younger children, Lydia, Ned, and Bobby. She wasn't sure she was up to the task.

At least Pa had gotten up this morning and gone to the barn with the boys to do chores. Maybe he was starting to come around and would help her more with the children now.

*****

"Can't we stop now?" Lydia pleaded. "My feet hurt awfully, and we've picked enough apples to feed the whole army."

"No," said Judith, although she sympathized with her little sister. The ladder rounds pressed painfully into her arches, too. "We have to pick every single apple as fast as we can."

The air was rich with the scents of sod, leaves, and ripe fruit. The sky held an intense blue that only came with bright autumn days. Judith had kept the children home from school for a second day to help with the harvest, and they had been at it all morning.

The three girls placed each apple carefully in the canvas bags that hung from their aching shoulders. When the bags became unbearably heavy, they emptied them gently into wooden boxes, wary not to bruise the apples. Meanwhile, Ned and Bobby picked up windfalls from the ground and plopped them into a barrel for cider making.

The next day their father would drive the apples to the railroad station in Oakland, where they would be sold, loaded into freight cars, and sent to the cities. Portland, Boston, New York. The barrels with the variety of apples stenciled on the tops would travel hundreds of miles, and vendors would sell the apples in produce markets and on street corners to people who never had the pleasure of picking fruit from their own trees.

Christina was working steadily, her mouth set in a grim line. Judith knew her shoulders ached as she reached again and again, grasping each apple and tipping it slightly, careful not to break off the spur that would bear next year's crop. Her younger sisters had worked diligently, and she was proud of them, but she knew they must not quit before the crop was in.

- 12 -

Pain stabbed between her shoulders. She went slowly down the ladder to empty her canvas bag.

"Judith!" Six-year-old Bobby's cry had an urgency that always made her heart trip. She whirled from the apple crate. The boy was backing slowly away from a well-fed Hereford steer.

"Make the cow go away," Bobby shrieked. The steer took a lumbering step toward him, and its long, pink tongue came out to lick Bobby's rumpled shirt. "Judith!"

"Ned," she called. "One of Mr. Thayer's cattle is loose."

Ned came running, and the steer jumped away, startled, then stopped a few yards away. He lowed as though offended and began to snuffle about in the grass for apples.

"Make him go home!" Bobby cowered behind one of the gnarled tree trunks.

Christina and Lydia began to shout their advice, but kept their perches on the ladders. Judith looked around and seized a broken branch. Cautiously she approached the steer.

"Move, you! Go home!"

Ned eased in on the other side, and the steer gave a snort and bounded a few yards toward Ben Thayer's fence, where his property bordered the Chadbournes'.

"Can you boys chase him home?" Judith asked.

"Come on, Bobby," Ned called, but his little brother whimpered and refused to leave his refuge behind the tree.

"I'll help him." Lydia climbed down the last few steps of her ladder and bounced to the ground. "Give me that stick. Move, cow!"

Ned grimaced. "He's not a cow. Don't you know anything? Besides, we don't want to make him run until we know where he got out."

Judith scanned the fence line and pointed. "It looks like the rails are down over there."

Ned became all business. "Right! Let's chase him through, Lydia. Then if we can't fix it, we'll have to get Mr. Thayer."

Judith sighed. "You two go on. Ned, if you have to run to Thayers', leave Lydia to watch the fence while you go. We don't want any more cattle in the orchard before we're done picking."

The two children hounded the steer until he waddled uncomplaining through the breach in the fence, then Ned set to work propping the downed rails into place.

"That should hold for a little while. I'll run up and tell Mr. Thayer when we go home for dinner."

"All right, if you think those cattle will stay put." Judith looked at the neighbor's lush pasture. Half a dozen fat steers grazed contentedly on the other side of the fence.

Bobby came to stand beside her. "Mr. Thayer ought to keep his cows home."

"They're not usually any trouble," Judith said. Thayer had lived next to them for nearly two years now, but he was not the typical Maine farmer. He pampered his animals with good feed and rich pasture. He ran a handful of cattle on a field twice the size of the pasture the Chadbournes' twenty Guernseys occupied. The errant steer must have smelled the ripe apples and found a weak spot in the fence. "Come on, we need to get back to work."

The diversion had given them all a short respite, but Judith was soon acutely aware of her aching muscles. The sun moved high overhead, and she forced herself not to think about her discomfort. Instead, she thought of Joel, who had been gone more than two weeks now, and their father. Pa hadn't seemed to care whether the apple crop was harvested or not, but she had wheedled a promise from him. He had stayed back at the house this morning, but he had assured her that he would sort the best of the Wolf River, Milton, Stark, and Jonathan apples into barrels and seal them for shipping and then take them into town.

Judith hoped he would follow through. She couldn't do it herself. She wouldn't have the strength to load the barrels in the wagon, even if she had time. She never seemed to rest anymore. Caring for the family and the added farm work left her exhausted each evening.

It was close to noon, and her empty stomach rumbled.

"Why don't you take Lydia with you and get dinner?" she said to Christina, as she moved her ladder around the tree.

"Are you sure?" Christina sounded relieved, but cautious, as though she didn't want to take the easy way out.

"Go." Judith glanced at Lydia, whose shoulders drooped beneath the thin calico of her everyday dress. "This work is too hard for her."

When Christina and Lydia had set out up the slope toward the farmhouse, Ned came and took over Christina's ladder. At eight, he was still round-faced and innocent, but Judith felt he had taken on worry beyond his years, trying to fill Joel's shoes and bear an extra share of the farm work these past few weeks.

"Why doesn't Father help us?" he asked, climbing nimbly to the top of the ladder and stretching his arm to its longest for a shining apple. "He always helped us before."

Judith sighed, at a loss for an answer. Since July, Pa not only neglected the farm work, but it seemed he hardly noticed the children. She thought they were over the worst of it now. Those first few weeks after Mother's death, when he'd seemed unaware of his surroundings, had terrified her. He was somewhat better now, resuming some chores, but with Joel away, the farm work threatened to overwhelm the family.

Joel had shouldered the burden manfully until he left for Lewiston. His example had bolstered Judith to do her part and more. She still couldn't understand why he'd been drafted when it seemed the Allies were on the verge of signing an armistice.

The eldest at twenty-one, Judith had given up her teaching job when her mother died. Her responsibilities now included caring for the children, doing the cooking, housework, and laundry, and tending the vegetable garden. She had helped the two younger boys trample down countless loads of hay this summer, compacting it on the wagon, as Joel and Christina pitched forkfuls onto the growing stack.

Joel had left with regret, but resigned to doing his duty. He wasn't as excited about it as Harry. His letters came faithfully. The green troops wondered if they would be sent to Europe to fight or to enforce peace terms. So far, Harry's unit was still in camp, and Joel hoped they would serve together when they went overseas.

For the past two weeks, Judith and the younger children had split up Joel's work. She and Christina took turns helping with the milking. There were only six cows producing milk now. The haying was over before Joel left, but their other crops had to be stored for the winter. Judith and Christina had canned hundreds of quarts of corn, tomatoes, green beans, and pickles. The younger children had heaped bins in the cellar with potatoes, beets, carrots, turnips, squash, and pumpkins.

Cash from the apple crop was the biggest part of the family's income, but there were other money-making ventures Judith couldn't neglect. She made butter to sell, but not as much as her mother used to make. They had a few steers and chickens that could be sold for butchering, and eggs and milk. Dry beans were stacked in the barn, still in the pods, waiting to be threshed. All winter long, people would stop in the dooryard to buy a few pounds of beans, and Judith would weigh them out on the scale on the front piazza. Kidney beans, pea beans, yellow eyes, sulfur beans, and Jacob's cattle. People knew the Chadbournes had good beans. The routine would go on, in spite of Mother's absence and the family's grief.

She looked up at the sun once more and decided they needed a rest. "Come on, boys. Let's go get lunch. And Ned, don't forget to go tell Mr. Thayer about the fence."

\*\*\*\*\*

That afternoon the children returned to the orchard under Judith's care. Their father had roused himself to load the wagon. He headed for the depot in Oakland with eight barrels of apples, taking Bobby with him.

Thankful for this encouraging sign of activity on his part, Judith drove herself and the other children to finish the picking. The fair weather held, and she was grateful for that.

From a distance, she saw Ben at work on the boundary fence. Ned waved to him, and he waved back but kept diligently at his task. She had half expected him to hire someone to do the work, but he seemed to know what he was doing. The next time Judith looked toward the fence, he was gone.

In the twilight, they stripped the apples from the last tree. Weary beyond words, they plodded toward the house. Father had returned from town and put the horses away.

"The army wants butter," he said when Judith staggered into the kitchen. "How much do you have on hand?"

"Only fifty pounds. I could have made more, but there wasn't time." She took out a knife and a sack of potatoes and began peeling them for a late supper.

"Wrap it all, and I'll take it in tomorrow," he said.

"But we're out of butter paper. I don't think there's a sheet left." Judith opened the drawer where her mother kept the supply of nine-by-seven sheets of waxed paper, but there was none.

"You'll have to go to Thayer's early to get more."

"I have to milk in the morning—" Judith began, but it was futile to try to reason with her father. He had walked out the back door, a milk pail in his hand. At least he wasn't sitting in the rocking chair, brooding.

Christina hurried past her, darting a worried glance at Judith as she threw on her old barn coat. Judith hated to send her out to the barn with Pa. He would feed the stock in silence, performing his evening chores by rote, then join Christina for the milking, sitting mutely on his three-legged stool. When they were finished, they would bring the milk into the house for Judith to strain. She would pour it into five-gallon cans in the cellar, where it would cool until the dairy wagon came the next morning.

She bent wearily over the sideboard, mixing the biscuit dough for supper and keeping an eye on the meat sizzling in the skillet on the stove. Her shoulders still ached. She heard silverware clink as Lydia moved slowly around the dining room table, setting six places. After sliding a large pan of biscuits into the oven, Judith primed the pitcher pump at the end of the iron sink and pumped a kettle full of water. She strained to lift it to the back of the wood range, where it would heat for washing the dishes.

She wondered suddenly where little Bobby was. Even the boys were tuckered out by the long day's work, but Ned would be in the barn, helping throw hay to the cows. She went to the dining room doorway.

"Have you seen Bobby?" she asked.

Lydia nodded toward the front room, and Judith stepped to the doorway. The little boy lay stretched out on the sofa, his mouth open and his eyes closed. His dark hair lay in disarray against the bolster Aunt Sarah had stitched. He looked like Father. Bobby, Ned, and Christina all had the dark, unruly hair and brown eyes of the Chadbournes, while she, Joel, and Lydia had inherited Mother's deep golden hair and gray-blue eyes. Bobby's long lashes lay against his tanned cheek, and in repose the active little boy seemed sweetly incapable of misbehaving. Judith smiled and went back to the kitchen.

She would have to go for the butter paper after milking in the morning, then prepare the butter for sale, set milk for cheese, and churn more butter. In the afternoon, she would work on the mending and ironing she had neglected during the apple harvest. Ned's trousers all seemed to be giving way at the knees, and Christina's school dresses were far too short. Her old teaching job looked easy now, in perspective.

Still, a shiver of anticipation went through her at the thought of visiting the handsome but mysterious printer's house. She'd heard so many stories, she couldn't help being eager to find out if they were true.

# Chapter 3

Judith rose at five the next morning and built up the fire in the cookstove. She milked by lantern light with her father, thankful that he had risen and not left her to milk the six cows alone. After that, she went in to help Christina get breakfast. After everyone had eaten, the children set off to school under Christina's watchful eye. Ned was usually reluctant to go to school, but after the hard work in the orchard, he was willing to go back to his books. The small high school classes met in a wing of the same building as the elementary school, so Christina would be with them all the way.

It was still early, not eight o'clock, when Judith finally left home and approached the Thayer house, holding a wool cape close against the October chill. Father had gone to the barn to pack more apples. She hoped he would have another load ready to go that day, along with her butter.

She was glad the youngsters were all able to continue their schooling. After Mother died, Christina had wanted to quit school and find a job, but Joel and Judith had insisted she take her last year of high school. She would graduate young, barely seventeen. Christina was so bright, Judith had hoped to see her go off to college, but that seemed impossible now. Even so, Christina must at least finish high school.

Judith turned in at Ben Thayer's driveway, noting his neatly kept yard and freshly painted outbuildings. He had money, and he didn't need to farm, but he puttered at raising beef and potatoes. He hired a man to cut hay for him.

His real business was printing—though she wasn't sure he needed a business. Maybe he saw it as a hobby. What had been the dining room when the Drakes owned the house was now his print shop, and the den had become his office. He printed butter paper, handbills, pamphlets, and billing forms for the telephone company. But in Judith's mind, he was an artist.

Joel had been to the house several times since Ben Thayer bought it, and she supposed her parents had, too, but Judith had not. She remembered it as a plain little farmhouse from the days when the Drakes owned it. She'd heard tales of wonderful paintings that now lurked in unexpected places, and she felt she was in for a treat.

She walked quickly up his long gravel driveway, between tall maple trees that flamed red and orange, with some that faded through peach to yellow. She wished she could paint like Ben Thayer. She would try to capture the brilliant colors of the foliage and hang them on the bedroom wall, where they would cheer her through the bleak Maine winter.

For at least five months of the year, her world was black and gray and white. The snow-covered fields, the overcast sky and the frozen river pressed in on her without relief. In late March or early April, the sky would brighten to blue. Just when she grew certain she couldn't take one more day of snow and ice, brown mud would break through on the driveway, and the river would open. Then, ever so slowly, a hundred shades of green would push their way out, and the myriad colors of flowers and birds would follow. Then Judith's heart would lift, and she would feel vibrantly alive again.

An artist, though … an artist must feel that way all the time. He kept the colors in his heart, and brought them out whenever he pleased.

Ben's house was trim and snug, painted white, with neat black shutters. He had hired Joel last spring, with two other boys, to paint it. Joel had been happy to earn some extra money in the week he worked there, but he had gained more than his wages.

He had come home in the evenings eager to tell Judith about what he had seen there: the printing press, and Ben's artwork. Ben was working on an intricate drawing of a Victorian mansion with ivy twining up the porch pillars. Each shingle had been distinct, Joel said, and the windows gleamed, although they were nothing but ink on paper. The leaves were so real you felt you could reach out and pick one. Judith wished she could have seen that drawing.

From then on, Joel had found excuses to visit Ben often. Ben had hired him for odd jobs whenever he wasn't busy at home. Joel whistled a lot, and related bits of stories Ben had told him, trying to repeat the man's exact words. Ben Thayer had become a hero in her brother's eyes, and Judith wasn't sure that was a good thing. There was so much they didn't know about him.

She went up the steps to the front porch, her green wool skirt swirling about her ankles, and knocked timidly on the door of the glassed-in piazza. No one came, so she renewed her efforts, more loudly. Still no response. She gingerly turned the doorknob and stepped inside.

She looked around the porch. Over the door that led to the house, a train of mules was painted in marvelous colors. Laden with heavy packs, the animals wound their way up a treacherous mountain slope. A bookcase stood in one corner, filled with classics and agriculture books. On the end panel of the shelves, two painted squirrels scrambled nimbly up the trunk of a beech tree. Judith smiled in delight. They exuded energy, and she almost saw their whiskers twitch.

From within the house, she could hear rhythmic mechanical sounds. He was working the press. She knocked on the inner door and jumped at the loudness of it. The measured churning stopped, and a few seconds later the door opened.

"Miss Chadbourne! A pleasure," said Ben.

His curly brown hair was short and crisp, and his vivid blue eyes scared her a little. His contagious smile made him look quite young.

"Good morning, Mr. Thayer," she said, returning the smile. "We're in need of butter paper."

"Well, I have two hundred sheets on hand."

"I'll take that now. My father told me to ask for a thousand sheets. Could we get the rest later?"

"Of course. Do you want it imprinted with your name?"

"Oh, I don't know," Judith said uncertainly. "It this something new?"

"Yes, half a cent more per sheet, but with *Wesley S. Chadbourne, Sidney, Maine,* on every one. It's good advertising. Could mean a lot more orders for butter."

Judith shook her head. "I'm afraid I couldn't handle more orders just now. The Army is buying every pound we can produce."

"Ah. Then that would be a waste of money. Perhaps later, after the war ends."

Judith nodded, not sure whether he was laughing at her or not.

"Won't you step inside, Miss Chadbourne?" He opened the door wide and gestured with an inky hand for her to pass him.

She went warily through the doorway and turned toward the office.

"Oh, it's in the print shop. This way."

She looked around furtively as he led her through the parlor. The furniture was modest but looked comfortable. She recognized two large armchairs and a green brocade sofa as having belonged to the Drakes. He had added more bookcases and two side tables with kerosene lamps. It was a little dusty. Mrs. Drake would never have allowed the dust to accumulate.

Inside one of the deep window frames, Judith glimpsed a morning glory vine climbing toward the ceiling. She caught her breath at the realism of the painted blossoms and wished she dared step closer to examine them.

The printing press dominated his shop, and divided wooden trays held type on a cherry sideboard. Several metal plates and tools she didn't recognize lay on a drop-leaf maple table. Cartons of paper sat on the floor under it. She crinkled her nose at the smell of the ink, mingled with wood smoke and coffee. At school, she always enjoyed the "new book" smell, but she wasn't sure she'd want to live with it continuously.

"Sorry about the fence incident yesterday."

"Oh, don't mention it." Judith felt her face flush for no good reason. She hoped Ned had been polite in delivering the news.

Ben opened an armoire that stood between the windows overlooking the pasture. Through the casement, Judith could see several plump, white-faced Hereford cattle standing tails to the wind, chewing peacefully.

"Here you go. I'll wrap it up for you." He produced a length of brown paper and plopped a pile of butter wrappers on it, then folded the edges up around the pile.

As he reached into the armoire for a ball of string, it occurred to Judith that she shouldn't be alone in the house with the man. Mother had drilled the rule into her head: a lady never ventured into a single man's lodgings alone. Perhaps she should have insisted that Pa complete this errand.

She looked uneasily over her shoulder. It was business, after all. Wouldn't it seem rude if she insisted on waiting on the porch?

There was no Mrs. Thayer, Judith knew. When he had moved to the neighborhood, the question had been whether or not there had *ever* been a Mrs. Thayer. So far as she knew, none of the local busybodies had uncovered the answer, although Christina had come home from school one day shortly after Ben's arrival, full of rumors and speculation. "Gladys says Mr. Thayer's wife died in the San Francisco earthquake in aught-six," she had declared, "but Grace says he's not old enough for that. Anna Baxter says he was never married, but his betrothed was drowned in the Charles River in Boston, and Mr. Thayer nearly drowned himself, trying to save her."

"Nonsense," her mother had replied. "You shouldn't listen to such gossip. Mr. Thayer is a decent man, and it's none of you girls' business if he ever had a wife or not."

So far as Judith could tell, he *was* decent. He attended the community church every Sunday morning and most Sunday evenings. The Chadbournes didn't usually make it to the midweek prayer meeting—never, in fact, since Judith's mother had died—and she didn't know if Ben Thayer went or not. He attended community events and seemed to have the respect of the town officials and farmers. She knew he and Dr. Stearns were friends. He wasn't what she would call outgoing—didn't stand around after church, talking to the other men. He was pleasant enough, though, and seemed capable of talking easily to anyone about any topic. Except his own history.

Judith looked around while his back was turned, noticing a cup of steaming coffee on the bench beside the printing press. Over the sideboard hung a matted pencil sketch of the capitol building in Augusta, and on the drop-leaf table lay a stack of newly-printed billing forms.

"Here you go." Ben held out the brown paper package, and she took it from him.

"Oh, I forgot—" She looked around for a place to set it down, then awkwardly handed it back to him. "If you would please—" She rummaged in her skirt pocket and brought out a dollar bill.

"Oh, thank you," he said, as if it weren't really necessary. "Tell your father about the imprints. You could have the farm name put on the butter paper, too. River Rest, isn't it?"

"Yes."

"A soothing name."

Judith couldn't help wondering how appropriate the name was. "My mother chose it when she and Pa moved in. We do have a nice view of the river, but we don't seem to get much rest."

Ben smiled sympathetically. "You've been working hard this fall, I guess."

"Well, yes." She looked up at him, wondering how much to say. "You've heard that Joel is gone to the camp?"

His eyes darkened. "Yes. I'm sorry. I had hoped your family would be spared."

"He took it well," Judith said.

Ben nodded. "He came to see me before he went. He asked me to look in on you folks, actually. I regret to say I've been remiss in that."

"No need. You're busy." She hesitated, longing to talk to someone about her brother. Her father was so taciturn lately, she hated to ask him anything. But Ben seemed to be a man who would know things, and she gathered her courage. "Do you think they'll send him across?"

"I don't know. We sent two hundred fifty thousand men last month. I suppose, until the Germans give up, we've got to keep up the pressure."

She nodded, her hope that Joel would soon be home fading. It could be months before an armistice was reached, and even then, the troops would be needed for some time.

*****

Watching Judith's anxious face, Ben felt he should have done more to encourage his neighbors after Mrs. Chadbourne's death. And Joel had asked him to keep an eye on the family, but he'd neglected that duty. The boy had been a bright place in his solitary life, and he deserved to have a friend keep his promise. He eyed Judith cautiously. "How is you father doing now? Is he any better?"

As Judith hesitated, he sensed that she was struggling with a private, frightening thing.

"Some. At least I hope he is." She looked up at him at last. "I've worried about him, Mr. Thayer."

"I know you have. I have prayed for him, that the Lord would bring him back to you."

"Thank you." She lowered her lashes, hiding her troubled eyes. "He seemed for a while to have given up completely. But he's more alert now, and he's getting up in the morning to do chores."

"That must be a relief, now that Joel is gone."

"Yes." She looked up, and her vulnerability caught at him. How could he not have noticed her before? She was beautiful in her earnestness. Her eyes were gray today, but sometimes they were blue, like her mother's had been—reflecting her surroundings or the weather? She'd been away from home last year, he knew, teaching a country school. Before that, she had just been one of the Chadbourne girls, on the verge of his consciousness when he drove past their farm, or when the family entered the church together. Suddenly she was struggling for her own identity in his mind, and he knew he would no longer think of her as Joel's older sister.

"I'm sorry," he said, trying not to stare at her stupidly. "I'll keep the guns as long as you think it's wise."

"I don't think he's missed them, and he doesn't hunt much anymore." She gave a courageous little shrug. "He seems to have perked up a little this past week or so. He took a load of apples into town yesterday, and wants to take more today, along with my butter." She gave a sudden start and reached for the parcel. "I need to get home and get it weighed and wrapped."

"Come back tomorrow or Friday. I'll have the rest of your butter paper ready."

"All right. Thank you." He walked beside her toward the front door. As they passed through his parlor, she threw a swift glance toward the morning glory window and stopped in mid-stride. He could tell by the sudden light that fired her eyes that she had spotted his artwork. He stopped, too, waiting for her reaction.

"I'm sorry." She looked up at him, and a flush spread over her face. "I saw the flowers there by the window when we came in, but I just noticed the hummingbird. It's—"

Ben found he was eager to learn what she thought. She seemed to be groping for the right word. Delightful? Beautiful? Inspiring? She didn't dredge it up, but the awe in her expression was enough. He smiled, satisfied. Her expressive lips began to curve upward.

"Thank you," he said. "It's something I did on a whim a couple of weeks ago. The flowers outside were fading, and I wanted some color."

"Yes." She stepped nearer the window and looked closely at the tiny green and red hummingbird that hovered among the bright painted blossoms. Ben stepped up beside her.

Could she understand how he had felt when the colors of the world outside began to fade? Every year when winter approached, it reminded him of the bleak coldness in his heart. He'd had enough of that, and wanted to stave it off, to infuse color and warmth into his life again.

Could she see the brush strokes that formed the feathers on the tiny wing? Her gaze traveled slowly up the twining stem of the morning glory vine, pausing on a blue flower with a white-streaked center. The blossoms seemed as though they had grown there, two dimensional, a freak of nature, but still natural. Sometimes it amazed him that God had given him the ability to duplicate nature so deftly. He hadn't thought another person could see his art that way, though.

She jumped a little, as though she realized suddenly that he was standing very close to her and felt uneasy. He stepped a little away. He wouldn't want to scare her off.

A movement beyond her drew his glance out the window. A wagon pulled by a chestnut gelding was coming smartly up the road.

"There's Albert Bond," he said with chagrin, "and I haven't finished his order yet."

"Forgive me," Judith said, "I've taken too much of your time."

"Not at all." He walked with her to the front door, wishing she would stay longer. Bond's wagon turned in at the bottom of the driveway as Judith left the house.

As Ben watched her trudge down the driveway in her drab brown cape, he wished his printing was finished for the day. He had the sudden urge to paint again, something delicate and subtly beautiful. Birds. He loved to paint birds, from the modest little phoebe to the flamboyant tanager. But they would have to wait.

\*\*\*\*\*

Albert Bond passed Judith halfway up the drive and lifted his hand in greeting. Judith waved, hoping he noticed her parcel. She felt herself blush again, just from the thought that Mr. Bond might think she had been indiscreet.

She quickened her steps, hoping her father would not be angry with her for taking so long to get the butter paper. The wind had picked up, and leaves swirled down from maples, poplars, and elms as she strode toward home.

She needn't have worried. Her father was sitting in his rocking chair in the front room, rocking slowly, his eyes unfocused.

"Pa?" she asked, setting the package down. She pulled off her cape.

He didn't respond.

"Pa." She stepped in front of him, speaking more sharply. He looked up at her, but kept rocking.

"Did you get the apples ready?"

He stirred a little.

"I'm going to wrap the butter so you can take it to town," she said.

"Don't know as I can do it today."

"You must, Pa. The army buyer needs it, remember? You're taking it and another load of apples."

He sighed, then heaved himself up out of the chair. Judith hurried to the kitchen and put on her apron. Christina and Lydia had done the breakfast dishes before they left for school, so at least she was spared that task.

She went carefully down the steep cellar stairs, carrying the package of paper, and uncovered the tub of butter she had churned. She reached for a paddle and a mold, and began shaping the butter into bricks. After weighing each one, she wrapped it carefully in Ben's paper. *Pure Butter*, it said, *one pound*. She imagined sheets that said *River Rest Farm*. It pleased her somehow, but it would be silly to spend twice as much for a name.

She worked diligently, though her shoulders began to ache again. She was not yet rested from the heavy work in the orchard, but she couldn't stop. She wondered if her father had gone out to the barn, or had sunk back into his chair.

At last she climbed the stairs, carrying a box full of wrapped butter. To her relief, Pa was not in the front room. She put on her cape and carried the box to the barn.

Her father was there, tamping the head onto a barrel. Crates of apples the children had picked were stacked high beyond him.

"Miltons?" Judith asked.

"Yes. Can you label it?"

She set the box of butter in the back of the wagon and went to where several brass stencils hung on the wall. She lifted down the one that said, *Milton Apples*.

"You should put your name and address on them, too," she said.

"This is all the buyer needs to know."

From a cupboard between the studs in the barn wall, Judith took a small can of paint and an inch-wide brush and took them to the barrel.

"Ben Thayer says it's good advertising. On the other end of the line, in the city, someone will see it. They'll know you have good apples, and if they know where to reach you, they might ask for more."

Her father grunted. "We never have any trouble selling our apples." He began sorting another crate, putting the best apples gently into the next empty barrel.

Judith opened the paint can and dipped the brush. As she carefully applied the blue color to the cutouts in the stencil, she pictured Ben delicately stroking in the veins on the morning glory leaves. And the lifelike little hummer. How had he captured it so perfectly with his paintbrush? She wondered if he had truly painted it for himself, or if he had hoped someone else would find it.

Now that she had seen part of his house, it was more mysterious in her mind. What magical sights were in the other rooms, where she had never been? Did he leave secret little masterpieces where no one else would ever see them?

# Chapter 4

On Friday morning, Judith sent the children to school and set about her baking. She was kneading bread when she heard an automobile drive in and went to the window.

Ben Thayer was climbing out of his car. Quickly she wiped her hands and removed her apron. Her father was outside somewhere, and she hoped he would appear to greet Ben before he made it to the front door, but he didn't.

She waited, heart pounding, until he knocked, then opened the door. Ben stood on the piazza holding a pasteboard box.

"Hello, Miss Chadbourne. I was going into town, and I had your butter paper ready, so I thought I'd stop in with it."

"Oh, please leave it right here." Judith stepped aside, and Ben brought the box in and set it down on the dining room floor.

"Thank you. I—I think my father is at the barn. I'm sorry, but I don't have any money in the house."

"No need to worry." He smiled easily. "He can pay me when I see him next. How are *you* doing?"

"Fine." She looked down at the skirt of her calico housedress. Her heart tripped rapidly, and unease nudged her because of his nearness. It was silly, really. He always behaved as a gentleman. She was an adult, had taught school successfully, and could speak with the minister or the postmaster coherently, without a blush or a stammer, but Ben Thayer made her feel awkward and naïve.

"Do you hear from Joel?"

"Yes, he's very good about writing. He thinks they may be transferred soon."

"Could I get his address? I'd like to send him a note."

"Yes, of course. Just a minute." She hurried to the front room, glad for an excuse to escape the scrutiny of those intent blue eyes. She opened her mother's desk, where they kept writing materials, and reached into a recess for the little notebook where her mother had kept addresses. As she pulled it out, it caught the edge of a tissue paper parcel and brought the small package with it, flinging it to the oak floor.

Judith moaned before the tinkling of shattered glass had died. She bent and opened the paper wrapping.

Bits of glass glittered in the sunlight that streamed through the window and threw rainbows on the ceiling. Judith stared at the splintered star ornament, beautiful even in its ruin. Tears filled her eyes and ran down her cheeks as she dropped to her knees.

"Had a mishap?"

She looked up. Ben was standing in the doorway, sympathy in his face.

Judith took a shaky breath. "It's—it's just—" She stopped, trying to rein in her emotions.

Already she had thought about Christmas, and how it would be without Mother. She was resolved to keep the family traditions going for the children's sake. If Father would bring in a fir tree, she would urge them to trim it with popcorn and paper chains, and then she had planned to produce their mother's precious ornament and hang it, as Mother had every year, from the highest branch.

Now the tradition would be only a memory. Judith realized her tears were not for the broken star, but for her mother and all her tender touches.

"—something of my mother's," she finished unsteadily.

Ben stepped forward and sank to one knee, surveying the slivers of crystal that had spilled out on the floorboards. "I'm so sorry. It was something beautiful." He looked at her keenly.

"Yes." Judith dashed the tears from her cheek with the back of her hand. "It was a star. A Christmas star made out of glass. My great-grandmother brought it from England." She stood. "I'll get the broom."

She hurried into the kitchen, where she dried her eyes on her apron before returning to the front room with the broom.

Ben still knelt, holding one of the larger fragments in his hand, examining it minutely.

"Here, let me." He stood and took the broom from her, sweeping up the slivers of glass that had escaped the paper when it fell.

When he handed her the dustpan, she carefully shook the shards into the paper and laid the parcel on the desk. She would show it to her father when she thought he was approachable, but she knew the star was beyond repair.

"Let me get the address for you." She hastily copied Joel's address onto a blank sheet of paper, noticing the flour stuck around the edges of her fingernails. Well, guests who arrived unannounced had to expect people to be busy. Ben had had ink on his hands when she had gone to his house on Wednesday. She turned and put the paper in his hand.

"I know he'd appreciate hearing from you," she said. "The boys get homesick, I think."

"I'm sure they do." He stood for a moment, watching her, and she felt the bothersome flush returning. "Is there anything you need in town? I'll be going to the post office and the grocery store."

"No, I don't think so, thank you."

He nodded. "Well, I'd like to talk to your father, if he's handy."

"I'm sure he's out around the barn somewhere." Judith looked out the window toward the barnyard.

"I'll just step out there." Ben went out and closed the door.

Judith watched him from the window for a moment. Having a man like Ben Thayer next door was becoming quite a distraction. Suddenly he occupied a great portion of her thoughts, and she was beginning to see why Joel liked him so much. In the past, she had equated his artistic bent to laziness, or at least boredom. But she was wrong about that. He was pensive, but he was also industrious and energetic. And he was considerate, stopping in with the paper and offering to run errands for her. She believed he truly cared about Joel's welfare, too. And those probing blue eyes!

She turned away from the window. It wouldn't do to let herself get all flustered when a neighbor dropped in on business. She had too much work to do to indulge in girlish reverie.

She took the paper and its shattered contents to the kitchen and put it in a high cupboard, inside a pie plate, then went back to her bread making.

When she set the dough to rise in the sun on the dining room windowsill, she looked out the window, past her bird feeder. Her father and Ben were leaning on the fence by the pasture, where the Guernsey cows were grazing. Pa was speaking seriously, and Ben was nodding.

She heard the car leave soon after. As she went about her housework, her thoughts went back over her conversation with Ben. Did he think she was foolish and clumsy? Did he think she worried too much? Did he think about her at all?

At noon, her father came into the house for his luncheon.

"Did you pay Mr. Thayer for the butter paper?" she asked.

"Yes." Pa asked the blessing, and they ate in silence. In the old days, Pa would talk and laugh at lunch, telling Mother how good the food was and discussing his plans for the rest of the day. The silence grew heavy, but Judith wasn't ready to tell him about the Christmas star, and she couldn't bear talking about Joel just then.

When she took away his plate and brought him a dish of bread pudding, he said, "I'll take the cider apples to the press this afternoon."

"All right."

"Judith, I'm afraid things are going to be tight this winter." He met her gaze for a moment, then looked away.

"How bad is it, Pa?"

"Pretty bad. If we'd had more butter, it would have helped. I didn't get but thirty dollars yesterday, between that and the apples."

It sounded like a meager sum to Judith, for all the labor they had spent. "Well, we won't starve," she said. "The cellar is full."

"Yes, but…"

"But what?"

"There are the taxes."

Taxes. Judith had never had to worry about taxes before. She knew her parents always scrimped and saved for a couple of months in the spring to have the payment ready when it was due on April first, but her father was worrying about it six months in advance.

"It's not until spring," she said.

"No, but I usually have most of the money in the bank by this time. I've let things go a bit, haven't I? I'm sorry, Judith." He sat with shoulders slumped, stirring his coffee.

"We didn't have to buy so much butter paper at once," she said. A thousand sheets. She had used fifty.

"We'll need it eventually. Besides, you'll need to keep selling butter, I'm afraid."

"But the cows are drying up, one by one."

He frowned.

She had been thankful when each cow went dry, because it meant that much less time spent in milking and churning. Her father usually managed to keep one cow fresh over the winter, ensuring a steady milk supply, but that was all they needed.

"And there's the fire insurance," Pa said.

She swallowed hard. "When is it due?"

"The fifteenth of November."

"How much?"

"Twenty-four dollars."

"Anything else?"

"Not now. There's always something, though."

She sat down opposite him. "Pa, should I have kept my teaching job?"

He sighed. "Don't know how I'd get by without you. The children and all. I just…haven't been able to keep up this year."

"But we'll be all right, won't we?" She thought of Uncle Peter, who had lost the old family farm, her great-grandfather's home place, twenty years earlier. He had let it go to rack and ruin, and had brought disgrace on the family when he had lost it for not paying his taxes year after year.

"That Ben Thayer." Pa shook his head unhappily.

"What about him?"

"He offered to buy this place. Offered me cash."

Judith stared at him. "You can't sell the farm!"

"No, of course not. I don't know what was in his mind."

She carried the dirty dishes to the kitchen and plunged them into hot water in the dishpan. Had she misread Ben so badly? She thought she saw empathy in his demeanor that morning. Was it really a calculating ambition? She counted over all the neighborly gestures. He'd dropped off the butter paper and inquired about the family. He wanted to write an encouraging note to Joel. He'd helped her clean up the broken glass. And now he wanted to buy their land, their home, the farm that sustained them. He wanted the property that bordered his. It didn't add up. A concerned neighbor wouldn't want to put a family out of its home.

*Have I been foolish to imagine he cared about us?* She scrubbed fiercely at the frying pan. There was no one she could talk to about this new, disturbing development. More than ever, she missed her mother.

\*\*\*\*\*

Ben frowned over his work, laying out the type for a handbill. He hadn't expected to be ambushed by his feelings— feelings he'd thought were long dead. He'd grown used to the solitude. Yes, he'd been lonely, but with no desire for companionship.

But now …

Judith was lovely, like the shy, graceful doe that edged out of his woodlot on quiet evenings. She held herself poised for flight, even while she went about her business.

She was so quiet he'd never noticed her until lately, but now it seemed he thought about her all the time. Her family's troubles had become a major concern. It wasn't really any of his business, but as a neighbor he might justify making it his affair. And he had promised Joel he would look in on the family now and then. But Wesley Chadbourne was too proud to accept help, too frugal to take a loan. Ben's suggestion of buying his farm had outraged him.

He never should have offered. It had seemed like a feasible plan at first. He would pay a good price for the place, enlarging his own holdings, and Wesley could move the children into town and find work there. It would be easier for them all. Less labor, fewer financial obligations, and Judith ... Judith would be free to get on with her own life.

But Wesley had recoiled at his suggestion, blasting Ben in his anger. He had bought the place years ago, as a home for his family, had poured his hard work into it. He was not about to relinquish it now.

And Judith was as stubborn as her father. She was timid in some ways, but she had the Chadbourne pride. No, there must be a better plan, one where the family could keep the farm and Wesley could keep his self-respect.

Ben straightened and stretched his arms. Perhaps it was good that Wesley had been riled at him. Maybe his anger would provoke him into taking better care of the farm and his children.

He walked into the parlor, where he lifted a delicate piece of glass from the mantle—one branch of Judith's Christmas star. He had pocketed the largest piece while she went for the broom. He held it in his palm, staring at it, trying to imagine the whole ornament, as it had been before she dropped it. He carried it into his office and sat down before his drawing board, placing the fragment on a clean sheet of paper. Pulling a magnifying glass from the desk drawer, he bent over the glittering piece of crystal. After half a minute, he reached for a drawing pencil.

# Chapter 5

Judith put Lydia to work churning butter on Saturday, while she and Christina cleaned the house and baked. Their father seemed to have shed his apathy. Perhaps Ben's proposition had shocked him out of it. He cut wood in the barnyard all morning, and Ned and Bobby stacked it in the woodshed. Judith drove herself to make the house sparkle.

"Why do we have to do all this every week?" Christina asked. "No one will see it."

"You never know who'll drop by. When they do, they won't be able to say the Chadbournes' home isn't clean, or that the children didn't eat as well as they did when their mother was alive."

By mid-afternoon, Christina was dragging around and moaning for respite. Judith had allowed Lydia to go to Aunt Sarah's to play with her cousins. At last she released Christina and sat down with her mother's mending basket. The boys' socks needed constant darning. She was exhausted, but she forced herself to keep working.

On Sunday, the family drove to church in the wagon under overcast skies. A chilly wind blew off the river. Father unhitched Chub, their gelding, in the churchyard and put him in the long row of horse sheds with a blanket over him. As she headed toward the church steps with the children, Judith met Ben.

"Miss Chadbourne."

"Mr. Thayer." It was the minimal civility. She tried to think what else to say to him, but was at a loss. Did she really want to be civil to him, after his insulting offer?

He smiled, seemingly oblivious to her cool demeanor. "I'm thinking of beginning a new venture, Miss Chadbourne. Perhaps it would interest you." He fell into step beside her.

"What is it?" she asked, her heart beating faster. What could he want with her? A new venture sounded exciting, but coming from him, the suggestion made her wary.

"It's a newspaper."

She thought about that. "There's a daily in Waterville."

"Yes, but country folk don't get into town to get it, and delivery is unreliable this far out. A lot of people can't afford to subscribe to a daily paper, anyway. I was thinking of a small, neighborhood weekly. I'd sell it for a nickel."

"Would that be profitable?" she asked doubtfully.

"Well, I wasn't thinking so much of profit."

She stared at him. "Why would you do it, then?"

"Oh, I don't know. Something to do. I thought Sidney people would like having their own paper with the local news."

"How would you even get the paper to print it on?"

"I've found a supplier."

Judith shook her head. Even the schools were short on paper these days. Thayer must have connections to be able to get newsprint so easily during wartime. She wasn't at all sure she wanted to trust him, and besides, it had nothing to do with her. "It sounds like a lot of work for nothing to me."

They were nearing the church door. Ben looked as if he would reply, but she nodded curtly and herded the children into the Chadbournes' usual pew, on the left side, halfway back. Her father came in and sat in the aisle seat, grim in his black suit. Ben settled himself across the aisle and a row ahead. Judith turned her eyes to the front and her thoughts to the service, but Ben Thayer and his new venture kept slipping into her mind. A newspaper, of all things. She supposed he could afford to do something like that. He had the resources to invest in anything that struck his fancy. If the enterprise was a failure, he would shrug it off and try something else.

She realized with a start that Christina was watching her, and that she had been watching Ben. She raised her chin and sat rigid, staring at the back of Orissa Grant's hat. Mrs. Grant wore the same black creation the year round, changing its adornments. For the month of October, it had a short veil and a ribbon rose. Judith knew that the Grants' son Spencer had gone into the army last spring. He was in Greece, or Crete, or some such place. She sent up a quick prayer for Joel, Harry, and all the other Sidney boys who had been drafted, then tried to concentrate on the pastor.

*****

On Wednesday, a knock came on the front door, and Judith looked out the window to see Ben Thayer on the front steps. She opened the door with a mixture of trepidation and delight. It felt a bit dangerous to find him on the doorstep when she was alone at home, but she didn't want to send him away. Of course, he was there on business with her father. He wouldn't come for any other reason.

The reminder of his last proposition to her father brought turmoil to her heart. She felt slightly guilty as she looked up into his eyes. She couldn't deny that he was a handsome man. And at some point, she had stopped thinking of him as part of her father's generation. Though he had to be past thirty, he was not so very far past, she was sure.

"Miss Chadbourne." His smile unnerved her further.

"Father has gone to the mill to get our cider," she said, before he could announce his purpose.

"I wanted to see you, actually."

"Oh." Her mind whirled and her pulse accelerated. She couldn't ask him in. The children were at school, and it would be all over the neighborhood if she invited a single man into the empty house. Just who would do the telling, she wasn't sure, but it would get around. Her mother had drilled her on such things since babyhood. "Just a moment, please."

She went quickly to the kitchen, where her cape hung on a hook by the back door. She threw it over her shoulders and went back to the front entrance, unable to imagine what he wanted to discuss with her.

"Would you like to walk in the yard?" she asked.

"That's fine."

She stepped outside with him. Neither his automobile nor his buggy was in sight, and she realized he had walked down from his house.

"Unless you're cold," she faltered.

"No, I'm warm enough, thank you."

They walked slowly toward the barn. Ben had his hands in his pockets. Judith wrapped her arms around herself under the cape. It was nearing the end of October, and they had frost nearly every night.

"Winter's coming," Ben said.

"Yes. I miss the leaves." The hardwoods were nearly bare, reaching long, thin fingers toward the brooding sky.

"Do you like the autumn?"

She shook her head, shivering. "It comes and goes too quickly. And I know what will follow."

He smiled at that. "We'll hope this winter is more cheerful than the last few. They say Turkey is near to surrendering to the Allies."

"Really?"

"Yes. I truly think we'll hear even better news soon."

"I pray you're right."

"I've decided to go ahead with the newspaper."

"Oh. I wish you success."

"I wondered if perhaps you would want to have a part in it."

She turned to face him in confusion.

"I don't understand. What could I do?"

"You could help gather the news."

"You mean, go around and ask people what's been going on?"

"Something like that. Report on Grange meetings and Ladies' Aid and other organizations. Write up a little story for each item. Compile interesting bits about who is visiting whom, and whose son is home on leave. Weddings and new babies. I'd pay you, of course."

"I couldn't possibly."

"No?"

"I wouldn't have time. I have all the work I can handle now, Mr. Thayer."

"I see." He was thoughtful. "I could pay you ten cents a column inch. You might make a good wage at it."

She shook her head. "You don't understand. I have the children to care for. That entails a lot of hard work. Cooking, laundry, cleaning, sewing. And I have to help Father with the milking, tend the milk, and make butter. There's so much to do, I haven't enough hours in the day. I couldn't possibly run around to Ladies' Aid meetings, even if you paid me by the hour."

He nodded. "It was just an idea. Think about it. If you change your mind, let me know."

Judith shook her head, though the idea did have some appeal. "I won't change my mind."

*****

For two weeks, she didn't see Ben except to nod at him across the church. Judith tried not to think about him, but often as she toiled over the laundry, she imagined Ben in his print shop, meticulously setting the type for Sidney's own newspaper. It would be interesting work, she thought, but what did it matter? She could never do something like that. Her work was clearly laid out for her here.

Joel's letters home were disturbing. An outbreak of influenza had spread through the camp at Lewiston. Sick men were quarantined, but the disease continued to spread. Judith prayed for her brother's health as she went about her ceaseless work. She was tired all the time, but lay awake nights wondering if Joel was safe and if Ben Thayer was really a friend. She never felt rested. She went on with her work, trying to ignore the fatigue.

The news of the war was encouraging, and at every gathering, there was talk of an impending armistice. But there was no word of the army coming home. The church women spoke longingly each week of possibly seeing their sons and husbands return for Christmas.

Her father sank once more into depression. He did the morning and evening chores, but spent most days sitting in his chair in the front room, staring. Judith tried to rouse him, but he ignored her efforts. When Joel's letters came, he would listen as she read them aloud, then sit rocking silently for a long time. Christina seemed to soak up her father's mood, becoming lethargic. She moped about the house and put off her schoolwork until Judith chastised her roundly.

Judith tried not to worry. There was nothing she could do to help Joel. Her family was another thing, though. If her father couldn't meet the bills, she would have to find a way to contribute some cash. In spite of her housework, she had to earn something.

She thought carefully about Ben's offer and decided that her first instinct was right. She could never work for him. She wasn't skilled at interviewing people, and seeing Ben often would be too stressful. But she knew she could teach. She enjoyed working with children, and she was especially good with the primary grades. It excited her to teach a youngster to read. Still, she hated the thought of leaving home again, and she wasn't sure the family could go on without her.

She began to make quiet inquiries about her options. One evening when the children were in bed, she confronted her father.

"We need to do something, Pa."

"What, child?"

"We need to discuss the family's needs," Judith said. "I think I could get a school after Christmas. The pastor's wife told me the teacher in West Sidney is leaving."

"But, Judith, you'd have to board over there!"

"I know, but you said yourself we need money for the taxes, and there are other bills. How else can we get the cash?"

Pa looked at her silently. She knew she was considered to be pliant; Christina was the headstrong one. But now Pa was leaving much of the work and the decision making to her, and she was becoming more assertive in her new role. Her father seemed troubled by that.

"You can't leave the children now. If Christina were out of school, it would be different. You're needed here, Judith, now that your mother's gone."

She swallowed, guilt-stricken by the pain in his expression. She had hoped deep down that he would tell her not to leave, but she couldn't see another way to solve their difficulties. Her many prayers seemed fruitless.

"Well, then, I'll stay. But I can't help wondering how we'll make ends meet."

Slowly he lifted his head and focused on her with a sigh. "That … is my worry. I'll find a way, Judith."

"But how?"

"I'll go to town tomorrow and ask about work at the shipyards."

Judith drew back a little and studied his face. "You'd have to go away."

"Better than you leaving the children right now."

She sent up a new prayer, lightning-quick. She was frightened for the family's future, but if her father saw his responsibility clearly, perhaps he would come out of his lethargy, even if it meant taking a demanding job a hundred miles away. She decided in that moment that she would not apply for the school position.

*****

On the twelfth of November, Ben Thayer's buggy tore into the dooryard at midmorning. Judith heard the horse's staccato hoofbeats and was at the door before he had leaped from the seat.

"Judith, the war is over! They signed the armistice yesterday." His face was radiant, his smile brilliant. "It's peace, Judith!"

She stood silent for a moment. It was not unexpected, and yet it was a shock. It had been so long, and times had been hard. She began to tremble, not because of the icy wind that tossed her hair.

"Are you sure?" she said at last, her bottom lip quivering.

"Yes! I've just come from town. Everyone is celebrating. It's really over." He smiled broadly. "I wanted to get the latest news on the local boys for the paper. I'm bringing out the first issue next week, and I thought I'd go to the store and call the commander in Lewiston to ask about Joel and some of the others. When I got to town, everybody was talking about it."

She put out her hand and grasped his sleeve. "Did you hear anything about Joel, Mr. Thayer? It's been five days since we heard from him last."

"Not specifically. The influenza is bad in the camp. The sickest men are being invalided out. The healthy ones will be sent on for active duty. We'll be sending fresh troops to Europe to clean things up while the peace terms are being settled. I couldn't get direct news of your brother. I'm sorry, Judith."

She turned away from him, leaning against the doorjamb and looking toward his buggy. Chester, Ben's liver chestnut gelding, was easing step by step toward the edge of the lawn, stretching his neck toward the dead grass.

She said shakily, "So Joel will probably be going overseas."

"But they won't be shooting at him," Ben said. "That's something, Judith."

"Yes." She looked directly at him then and realized his gaze was focused on her face, and that he was addressing her by her first name. It was unsettling, and she stood a little straighter and tried to put authority in her voice. "You must tell Pa the news. He's in the barn. He's going to Portsmouth to try to get work in the shipyard for the winter, and he's packing his tools. Do you—do you think they'll need men now, Mr. Thayer?"

"I wouldn't be surprised. They'll need the ships to bring our men home, and when everything is settled, some will be converted for peacetime use. I don't think the shipyards will shut down."

"I hope not," Judith said.

She and her father had talked long the night before. At last he had left his reverie and looked baldly at the family's situation. Finding work away from the farm was the only way he could see to bolster their strained finances. He had experience from working in the shipyard during the Spanish American War and had heard the yard in Portland was hiring skilled carpenters. He thought he could earn good wages and send them home to Judith over the winter months, when the farm work would be light. She was still uneasy at the thought of him leaving them, but relieved to see him taking charge of the family's welfare again.

"You'll be alone here with the children," Ben said.

She looked up, surprised at the gentleness in his voice.

"Yes, but I have aunts and uncles nearby to call on if I need help."

He nodded. "Well, I'm one of your nearest neighbors. I hope you will call on me if you are in distress."

"Thank you." She wasn't sure if she could ever bring herself to call on Ben. She wasn't sure yet that she could trust him completely, though his friendly overtures seemed genuine.

"Perhaps your father won't need to go now."

"The war being over won't save our farm, Mr. Thayer. If anything, we'll be worse off. The army won't buy up all our crops when the men have been discharged. No, if they'll still hire him, he has to go."

"Is your situation really so precarious?" he asked softly.

It wasn't polite to discuss one's finances, she knew, but when she looked up into his blue eyes her reservation faded. "I'm afraid it is. We can barely scrape up the insurance money. It's due in a few days. After that, well…there are taxes in the spring. Father says they'd put a lien on him for sure next year. We can't lose the farm, Mr. Thayer." She said it a bit fiercely, remembering he had offered a few weeks before to buy the place, although it had never been mentioned between them.

"I'm sorry. If there's anything I can do…"

"Pray that my brother comes home."

He nodded. "I will. Judith, the offer to work for the paper is still open."

"I told you I can't. Especially with father leaving."

"All right." He looked toward the barn. "I've got most of the material I need for the first issue, but I'll need someone to help me get the news after this. I'll go out some myself, but I'll still be running the print shop. I don't suppose—"

He hesitated, and she looked expectantly at him.

"I don't suppose your sister Christina could help me out? I really need a reporter."

"Christina? She's so young. And she has no experience whatever."

"I'll train her. I've been a reporter myself. I can teach her, I'm sure. She's bright." He watched her closely.

"I don't know. Can I think about it?"

"Of course. I wouldn't work her too hard, but she might be able to earn three or four dollars a week. If you decide it's all right, ask her. I'd like to know within a couple of days, though."

She nodded. "Please don't say anything to Pa about it."

"I won't. But I would like to speak to him about the armistice, and about Joel."

"Mr. Thayer—"

"Ben."

She halted on that, tried to say it, then skipped over it. "If Christina worked for you, how could you pay her? I just don't see that you'll make much on this weekly paper."

"I'll sell ads." He was apparently untroubled over the financing of the paper. "Maybe Christina could help with that end as well. I'd give her a commission."

"There aren't many businesses in Sidney," Judith said.

"There are some, and maybe a few in Oakland or Augusta would find it worthwhile to advertise with us. We can sell classified ads, too."

"Mr. Thayer—"

He looked at her sharply.

She tried to make herself say *Ben,* but it didn't seem right. She was twenty-one, and he was a near neighbor, but still. Mother had always called him Mr. Thayer.

"Yes?" he asked.

"You aren't just doing this…"

He eyed her narrowly.

"I mean, you offered to buy our farm. Now you're offering a job to me or Christina, with wages you won't realize from the business. It seems rather impractical to me."

"You don't think I can make a profit?"

"I don't know. I rather doubt it." She was blushing, and shivering at the same time. She hugged herself and avoided his penetrating gaze. When she sneaked a glance, he was smiling, but somehow he didn't look happy.

"I'll take that as a challenge," he said. "This paper will make a profit within a year."

"Or?"

"No *or.* It just will. That's a promise. Send Christina up to see me if she wants a job." He tipped his hat brim and turned away, striding toward the barn.

Judith closed the door and hurried back to the kitchen, where she added several split logs to the fire. Ben's look still troubled her. She wondered if he was angry with her, or just determined to prove her wrong.

# Chapter 6

Ben sat at his drawing board that afternoon, working on an illustration, but his mind was on Judith. She was not as meek as he had thought her. She had some fire in her, and, as he'd suspected, a touch of her father's obstinacy.

And she had her mother's deep golden hair and fine features. Mrs. Chadbourne had been a beauty before she became ill. Judith had inherited all the best from both sides, it seemed. He considered her father's tenacity to be an asset. Before losing himself in his grief, Wesley had been a real fighter. It could be irritating at times, but that was much better than his recent apathy. Ben was glad he was coming out of it at last.

"You're going into the shipyard in Portsmouth, I hear, Mr. Chadbourne," Ben had said in greeting when he entered the barn at River Rest.

"Yes, sir, I've got six children to provide for. One's away in the army, but I still have five mouths to feed. I've got the skill and the tools to do it with."

The old pride and bluster were back.

Ben sighed. It would be better this way, although it would be difficult for Judith to hold the family together all winter in her father's absence. He was glad Wesley had refused his offer on the farm. He didn't need more land, and he really didn't want the Chadbournes to move out of the neighborhood. He would have to make sure he performed his neighborly duties more conscientiously than he had in the past. Perhaps in time Judith would accept his friendship. He didn't dare hope for more.

A twinge of unfamiliar guilt began to nag him. If only Joel hadn't been drafted so suddenly. It wasn't his fault, but he couldn't help wondering if he couldn't have done something.

Somehow, he ought to have been able to go in the boy's place. He had no one depending on him. He wouldn't be missed, at least not the way Joel was missed. Poor Judith had lost her mother and her elder brother in quick succession, and now her father was leaving, too, although in an effort to provide for her and the younger children.

Ben and Joel had gone together to register. Why had Joel been drafted, and not him? If his own part in the war was to be here in Sidney, then Ben would do his best to be a comfort to some of the folk here. And he would look for ways to take up the slack for Judith, whether she admitted she needed help or not.

*****

"He'll pay me for this?" Christina asked incredulously that evening.

Judith had waited until they were alone. The three younger children were in bed, and their father had also retired early, planning to be up and off for Portsmouth at dawn.

"Yes. He says he will. How he'll get the money, I don't know."

"He has money," Christina said knowingly.

"You're listening to gossip again," said Judith.

"Maybe. But you said he'll pay me to do it."

Judith was troubled. "It's not gossip he wants."

"Sure, it is. He wants to print everything the people of Sidney want to know."

"Maybe this is not a good idea."

"I think it's a great idea." Christina's eyes sparkled.

"Let's sleep on it," said Judith. Somehow the newspaper business seemed vaguely dishonorable, at least for a woman.

"I want to do this." Christina's eyes held a spark of determination, and Judith wavered.

"If it seems reasonable in the morning, we'll talk to Father."

"Oh, let's not tell Father," said Christina.

Judith ignored the memory of her own plea to Ben to keep the proposal from her father. "Why not? You're afraid he'll disapprove? Maybe that should tell us something. Christina, we can't have people thinking you're a busybody."

"I won't be. I'll be a reporter, working in my official capacity. But Father's been so odd lately. He might refuse to let me, for no reason. If I can do this, and we can put the money aside, think how surprised he'll be! Judith, if he comes home at Christmas and we can show him that I've earned money, he'll be pleased, don't you think?"

Christina's desire to help the family was a less mature version of her own drive to keep the family going as her mother had, Judith realized. She reached for Christina's hand and squeezed her fingers.

*****

Pa caught a ride to the train station the next morning with Merton Hammond, who went once a week to Oakland, regular as clockwork. Judith and Christina kissed their father in the driveway and watched Hammond's wagon out of sight, then hurried to the barn to milk five cows and feed the stock.

Judith carried two pails of milk inside as Christina let the last of the cows out to pasture. She woke Lydia, Ned, and Bobby and began preparing breakfast.

Christina came in through the back door carrying more milk pails, and hung her barn coat on a hook.

"Shall I stop at Mr. Thayer's on the way home from school?" she asked.

"Absolutely not." Judith carefully measured oatmeal into the top of the double boiler.

"Why not?"

"You can't go to his house alone."

"Then how can I work for him?" Christina asked.

Judith stirred the oatmeal as she thought about it. "I'll go with you, and we'll discuss the job with him. If you can go out

- 50 -

and get the news and take it to him, just hand him your stories through the door, it should be all right."

Christina looked doubtful. "You're so prissy, Judith. Mr. Thayer's a good man. Wouldn't it be like going to work in a store or an office and having a man for a boss?"

"It's a little different when the office is in his house, and he's a single man. Mother wouldn't like it, I'm sure," Judith insisted.

"Mother isn't here."

"Exactly. I am in her place. You've got to go by what I say, Christina, or I can't let you do this. We've got to preserve our reputation."

"Reputation." Christina's lip crinkled in disdain.

"Yes. If that seems old fashioned to you, I'm sorry. You'll understand someday. Your reputation is one of the most valuable things you possess. You have to protect it."

Christina tossed her head as the boys noisily entered the room. "All right, but I'm going to do this, Judith. It's my first chance to earn hard cash, and I *will* do it."

Judith sighed.

"Judith, will you braid my hair?" Lydia asked.

At almost the same time, Ned said, "Judith, I can't find my speller."

She turned away from Christina. It was easier to meet the youngsters' immediate needs than to argue with Christina. When the children had left for school, she sat for a few moments, letting her mind rest. How had Mother done it? She'd done as much work as Judith did now, perhaps more, and she'd often sung cheerfully as she scrubbed the floor or folded laundry. Judith never felt like singing anymore. She hadn't the energy.

*****

Bud Hofses, the mail carrier, brought the mail later that morning. He always came around in his buggy when the roads were passable. Judith ran outside to meet him.

"It's official, Miss Judith," he said happily as he handed her two letters. "I'm getting a Model T next month."

"Really?" Bud had talked about it for nearly a year, but she hadn't expected him to actually buy one. So far, his spotted mare, Dolly, did the job.

"Uh-huh. Got to. They'll give the mail contract to someone else if I don't have an automobile. They say Dolly's too slow."

"I guess that's progress," Judith said. "Will you be able to get around in an automobile this winter?"

Bud grinned. "Not likely. Dolly will be pulling the sled."

"You shouldn't have to deliver the mail by sleigh. Why doesn't the post office give you an automobile?" she asked.

Bud slapped his knee. "That's a good one. Imagine, the government handing out cars to mail carriers."

Judith blinked. She hadn't thought it was that far-fetched. She looked down at the letters and smiled. "You've brought me something from my brother!"

"I hope it's good news." Bud lifted the reins. "Up, Dolly."

She read the letter to the children when they returned home from school that afternoon.

"We expect our unit to pull out soon," Joel had written. "Harry Gardner was taken by influenza yesterday. He is in the infirmary now. His unit left this morning. We don't know where they are going, and if we did, I couldn't tell you. Harry must be upset that he was left behind."

Judith watched Christina's face when she read the news, and saw her sister's eyes darken. Christina's attachment to Harry was a long-standing fact, and Judith could see that it troubled her to hear of his illness.

"I heard from Ben Thayer," Joel's letter went on. "He says you all are working hard to keep the farm in shape. When I come home, he says he'll teach me to drive. I wrote and told him Uncle Sam may beat him to it. A lot of us are going to be driving trucks. We'll see what happens. It could be a long time before I see you again."

Judith and Christina left the three youngsters eating cookies, with instructions to bring the laundry in from the clothesline afterward. Judith put on her heavy wool coat. Black gloves her mother had knit the winter before were in the pockets, and Judith felt a surge of love and loss as she pulled them on. Even now, her mother's work was protecting her, keeping her warm. She tied a scarf around her head and wrapped the ends around her neck.

Side by side, the two girls walked up the road toward Ben's house.

"Ladies!" Ben's pleasure was obvious when he opened the door. "Please come in. I hope this means I have a reporter."

He led the way into his office. Judith's eyes flew to the wall over the desk, and she caught her breath. A drawing of a waterfall hung there, and its beauty thrilled her. She and Christina took off their gloves and scarves and unbuttoned their coats. Judith glanced around the room. On the far wall was an ink drawing of a fox skulking on the edge of a farm lane. Pinned to a board on a small, slanted desk by the window was a pencil sketch of a man in a top hat prodding ineffectually at an elephant.

"May I take your coats, ladies?" Ben asked.

Judith hesitated, then took hers off. She had worn a blue plaid dress, better than her housedresses, but not her best. Christina still wore the gray skirt and white blouse she had worn to school.

"What's this?" Judith asked timidly, nodding toward the elephant sketch.

"Oh, that's Mr. Wilson," said Ben. "He's having a difficult time with the Republican Congress."

Judith wondered at his interest in politics. The election had passed without her giving it much thought. Her father hadn't bothered to vote, a first in his adult life, and he was the only male of age in the household. It was not the year for a presidential election, and the family's troubles were too pressing for her to think about politics.

"Is it for the paper?" Christina asked with interest.

"No, actually, it's for a magazine," Ben said.

Judith stared at him. "You draw cartoons for magazines."

"Sometimes. It pays the bills." He laid their wraps over a small table and motioned them toward chairs.

"So, Christina, you're interested in writing up news for me?"

"I'd like to try." She sat in the oak swivel chair before his desk, and Judith took the Windsor chair near the drawing board. Ben sat on the corner of the desk.

"All right, I'm printing the first edition Monday. I'll need all material for the second edition by next Friday. That way, I'll have Saturday to set type. I'll work on the major stories, editorials, and ads. I'll expect you to get the human interest news for me."

"What does that involve?" Christina asked.

"Well, on Saturdays and after school, you can go around and talk to people. Find out what's happening that will interest people. The more local names you can mention, the better."

"Like Harry Gardner having influenza?" Christina asked.

"Really? I'm sorry to hear that," Ben said.

"Yes, Joel wrote us," said Judith, "but isn't it rather inconsiderate to print news like that? Suppose you publish a notice of someone being ill, and then we hear the next day the person died. Wouldn't that upset the family?"

"Hmm, it's all subjective," Ben said. "I can see your point, but I think in that case the family would understand that we published the item with the intention of informing people of the health of someone they know and like. Perhaps we could even print Harry's address so people could send him cards. I tell you what, Christina. On the last possible day, which would be Friday, your deadline, drop in at the Gardners' and ask Harry's mother what the latest news is. If Harry's still ill, or recovering, we'll print it. If, heaven forbid, he's succumbed, well, that would go under obituaries, and I would go see Mr. and Mrs. Gardner and write it up myself."

Christina's face had paled, and she nodded solemnly. Judith wished Harry's name had never come into the conversation.

"I don't know," said Judith. "This is like prying into people's private lives."

"Not at all," said Ben. "Let's say you hear that your brother has been promoted. Wouldn't you want all the neighbors to know? What better way than to put it in the *Hummer*?"

"The *Hummer*?" Christina asked doubtfully.

"Sure," said Ben. "For hummingbird. It's going to be a small paper. I'm starting out with only four pages. It will be compact, but beautiful, adroit and lively. Also, we'll keep the news humming."

He was watching Judith, and she smiled, thinking of the little green and red hummingbird that hovered delicately over a morning glory on the woodwork in the parlor. He smiled back, and it was as though he read her thoughts. She looked quickly away, but their shared secret made her heart pound.

"Why not the *Eagle* or something more impressive?" Christina asked.

"You don't want to work for the *Hummer*?" Ben asked with mock indignation.

"I didn't say that."

He laughed. "All right, let me give you a rundown of the kinds of news I want. There's military news, of course, babies, weddings, betrothals, and anniversaries. Parties. Birthday celebrations, family reunions. Church news. You know, bazaars, public suppers. School news. You can check with the school office one day on your lunch break."

He went on, referring to a list he had written on a sheet of paper. Judith bent toward the sketch on the drawing board. In the lower right corner, near the elephant's hind foot, were the initials B.T. The thin, spectacled man was unmistakably the President. So this was how Ben really supported himself, not with investments or inherited trust funds or the haphazard income he received from his printing jobs. She felt better somehow, more sure of his character.

She watched his earnest face as he patiently went down the list. After they had covered all of the categories for news, he handed the paper to Christina and smiled. Judith's heart lurched unexpectedly, and she looked at her sister. Christina was still frowning over the lengthy list.

Ben sat back on the edge of the desk. "You'll do great, Christina. Don't forget, I need everything for the next edition by Friday afternoon, one week from today. Come here after school with it. If you have some news written up earlier, bring it to me anytime. The sooner the better."

"How do I write it?" Christina's voice squeaked a little, and Judith knew she was a little frightened, but excited. Christina was determined to succeed.

Judith sat quietly while Ben brought out several newspapers, copies of the Waterville daily and a weekly in Ellsworth. He pointed out several examples Christina could model her stories on, and a couple of items he thought were done poorly. Christina listened attentively.

"Tell you what," Ben said, "why don't you come see me after you get your first item, and I'll go over it with you. Don't wait until next Friday. If you pick something up tomorrow, bring it in."

Judith stirred uneasily, and Ben shot her a glance.

"Mr. Thayer," she began.

"Ben." He smiled.

Judith nodded deferentially. "It's just that I don't know as Christina should … come to the house alone. Our mother is gone, and Father's away now, and, well, I don't want people to talk."

Ben's brow furrowed. "I'm sorry. I never considered that to be a problem."

Judith struggled with her embarrassment. She didn't want him to think she didn't trust him, or that she was a hopeless Victorian. Her younger sister was more modern in her thinking, and she knew that her own prudence would be more than compensated by Christina's bold exuberance.

She cleared her throat and stared studiously at her folded hands. "I thought perhaps she could bring you her news and hand it to you at the door, but if you're going to have to consult…"

Ben looked at her blankly. "Miss Chadbourne—Judith—I assure you—" He paused, then switched approaches. "Perhaps I should come to your house tomorrow evening. I could go over Christina's items with her and take away any she has ready. Would that be acceptable?"

"I guess so." Judith looked at Christina, who nodded.

"I'm sure once she's done a few articles, she won't need constant supervision," Ben went on. "When she's confident, she can just drop her copy off with me as you suggested."

Judith stood, greatly relieved. "Thank you, Mr. Thayer." His eyebrows quirked, and she thought he would say *Ben*, but he didn't. "Which magazine will Mr. Wilson and the elephant appear in?"

"That's for *Uptown New York*."

She was stunned. She had heard of *Uptown New York*, of course, had even seen a copy once in the public library in town, and knew it was considered a rather highbrow publication. Not the choice of reading for most farmers. She wondered how much Ben was paid for such a simple drawing.

"You work for them regularly?" she asked, trying to sort out Ben Thayer in her mind.

He hesitated then smiled a little. "Well, I wouldn't publish it in the *Hummer*, but, since you ask, I was their art director for two years, and they've asked me to send them a drawing or two each month since I've moved to the hinterlands." He looked quickly at Christina then back to Judith. "That's between us. I don't want my neighbors to think I'm disdainful of the rustic life."

Judith wanted to ask him why he had chosen Sidney, Maine over the metropolitan lifestyle. She wanted to ask him a lot of things. She pulled her gloves on thoughtfully.

Christina was buttoning her coat, her face flushed with enthusiasm for her new adventure. "So I'll get all the news I can tomorrow and write it up, and you'll come by after supper and look at it," she said to Ben.

"Yes, I'll see you then." He walked with them to the door. "Any word from Joel?"

"Yes, we had a nice letter today." Judith looked cautiously at him as Christina bounced down the steps from the piazza.

"I've been praying for him," Ben said softly, so that only Judith could hear. "He's a smart young man."

"Thank you. I know he's in God's hands." A ray of comfort warmed her with his smile, and she found her reserve melting again. Joel liked Ben enormously, and she found she couldn't mistrust his air of calm solidity. His concern had to be genuine. He didn't want her father's farm. His offer had been an awkward way of trying to help them. Perhaps the newspaper was, too, but she wouldn't worry about that. He had taken an interest in her brother, and if he were doing this for Joel's sake, so be it.

# Chapter 7

Judith made Christina and Lydia help her clean the downstairs Saturday morning while the boys worked at cleaning out the barn. By ten o'clock, the kitchen, dining room and front room shone, and she let Christina hitch Lady to the wagon and start around the neighborhood. It still seemed rather forward for a sixteen-year-old girl to be approaching people and asking for news. Judith wished she had asked her father after all.

She set Ned and Bobby to stacking the last of the wood in the shed after lunch, and wondered if Father had cut enough. The logs had been felled the winter before and hauled out of the woods over the snow with the oxen. They were left to dry in piles behind the barn. Joel had begun the job of sawing and splitting them, but had left it unfinished when he was drafted.

Judith checked anxiously on the boys several times as they worked. If the winter was not too severe, she supposed they would have enough wood. But she wondered who would cut wood that winter for the next year.

Lydia helped her with the laundry and baking. They made bread, cookies, pies and raisin turnovers. The beanpot stayed in the back of the oven all day.

"We'll serve the turnovers tonight, when Mr. Thayer is here," Judith said as she took the last cookie sheet from the oven. She wasn't sure if pastry was quite the thing for a business meeting, but her mother had always offered refreshments to anyone who entered her door.

As she poured hot water into the dishpan to wash up the pans, Ned came in the back door calling, "Judith!"

"What is it, Ned?"

"Bobby's in the hayloft, and he won't come down."

"Why not?"

"He's crying. I told him to come in, but he won't."

- 59 -

"Are you done with the wood?"

"Yes, it's all in. Can I have some cookies?"

"May I," said Judith. "Yes, you may have two, with some milk. Lydia's probably ready for a break, too. I'll see about Bobby."

She put on her barn coat and said sternly, "Watch those pies, Lydia, and wash up the utensils after you have your snack. I'll be back soon." She made her way through the long corridor, an ell that attached the house and barn. As she came into the main barn floor, the smells of dry timothy hay, manure, and horses greeted her. She went past the horse stalls, onto the open floor between the horse barn and the cow stalls.

"Bobby?" she called softly. She listened, but heard nothing. A ladder went up to the haymow over the cow stalls. She wasn't sure if he was there, or in the large mow on the other side of the floor. She went cautiously up the ladder, clutching her skirt with one hand to keep from tripping herself, and raised her head above the level of the mow floor.

"Bobby?"

She heard a faint rustling in one corner, and squinted toward it. Her six-year-old brother was curled up in a ball, mostly covered with hay, his face turned away from her.

She stood there a moment, then gathered her skirts around her and climbed up into the mow. Her feet sank into the yielding hay as she lumbered awkwardly over the irregular, spongy surface toward her brother.

"Bobby," she said softly, sitting down in the fragrant timothy beside him and putting her hand on his shoulder. "What's wrong?"

He didn't answer, but sobbed quietly. Judith reached into her pocket for a handkerchief and held it out to him. He took it and wiped his face, but didn't look at her.

She pulled him toward her and held him in her arms, and his crying broke out again, louder than before. Judith sat for a long time, rubbing his back a little and letting him cry. The animals were all out to pasture, and the barn was quiet except for Bobby's weeping. At last the storm subsided, and he sat leaning against her, breathing raggedly.

"What is it?" she asked again.

"I just … miss Mama," he said at last. He dabbed angrily at his eyes with the handkerchief.

Judith hugged him, tears springing to her own eyes. She had been so busy, worked so hard. She had thought Bobby might be too young to understand how disconsolate and alone she had felt when their mother died, but perhaps the void was even greater for the boy. She had had twenty-one years with her mother to treasure in her memory. She would never forget her dear face, her gentle touch, her musical voice. Bobby had far less, and as he grew up, his memories of Mother might grow dim.

"I do, too," she said brokenly. They clung together. "It's all right to cry, honey. I do it myself."

"Sometimes I think I'll go in the kitchen and she'll be there," he whispered.

"I know. I feel that way, too. You come to me when you feel that way, Bobby. I'll be there."

He sniffed and took a final swipe at his nose, then smiled up at her sheepishly. "I don't like it when I cry."

"Me either, but I usually feel better afterward."

He scowled over that. "Ned makes fun of me."

"Well, he'd better not. Even grownups cry when something this sad happens."

"Even Joel?"

"Yes." She remembered all too keenly the night last summer when she had found Joel sitting on the back piazza steps, his head in his hands, sobbing. It was the only time she knew of that he had broken down. The weight of responsibility had threatened to crush him. That was the night they had really thrashed out their options for the family, and Judith had known she had to give up teaching and stay home with the children.

She looked down at Bobby and stroked his dark hair. "Lydia and Ned are eating cookies. Do you want some?"

Bobby nodded.

"Come on."

Bobby crawled nimbly to the ladder and was down it in a moment. She followed slowly and paused at the top of the ladder. Bobby was looking up at her with large, dark eyes. "Come down, Judith."

She laughed as she carefully went down. "It's been a long time since I've been up here!" She joined him on the barn floor and picked a wisp of hay from his hair, then brushed her coat and skirt with her hands.

"Come on. I made sugar cookies, and Lydia made ginger snaps."

"Oh, boy!" Bobby ran ahead of her through the horse barn and down the ell to the house.

*****

Bud Hofses had been there while she was in the barn. Lydia held up a letter as Judith hung up her coat.

"It's from the Army." Lydia's voice caught a little. "Can we open it? It's addressed to Father."

Judith took the envelope and looked at it, fear rising up inside her. Camp Commander, Lewiston, Maine. The address was typed. She looked guardedly at Lydia, and Lydia was still watching her.

She set the letter on the sideboard carelessly. "I'm ready for a cup of tea."

"Aren't you going to open it?" Ned asked, his eyes large.

"Maybe later," Judith said, as casually as she could. She put tea in the perforated metal ball and poured water from the kettle over it, in her mother's china teapot. "So, the pies are out?" She looked at the four brown-crusted pies cooling on racks on the table.

"Yes," Lydia faltered.

"That's good." Judith poured her tea deliberately, sat down and reached for a gingersnap. "Your cookies are delicious, Lydia."

She saw a glance pass between Ned and Lydia. Bobby was oblivious, drinking milk from his special tumbler, the one with cowboys painted on it.

She sent them all out to bring the livestock into the barn and looked at the clock. Christina should be home. With dread she walked to the sideboard by the cast iron sink and picked up the envelope.

*Dear Lord,* she prayed, *I'm afraid of what I might read here. Please, keep my brother safe!*

Very slowly, she loosened the flap of the envelope.

Christina came in a few minutes later, excited about her success in gleaning news from the neighbors. Judith shooed her into the front room to write up her articles while the material was fresh in her mind. She put several potatoes in the oven and went to the barn.

Ned had herded the cattle into their stalls, and Lydia closed the Dutch door on Chub's box stall. Bobby was in the second box stall with Lady, stroking as high as he could reach on the mare's flank with a soft brush.

Judith called the children to her and explained that Christina needed some quiet time to complete her work for Mr. Thayer.

"We can do the chores without her tonight," she assured them. "Bobby, you help Lydia get hay down. Lydia, can you get the horses' oats? Ned, I think it's time you had a milking lesson. You're big enough."

It took longer than usual, but when the stock was fed and the milk cows stripped, they trudged into the house to find that Christina had put carrots on to boil and was slicing ham into the frying pan.

"I got my news written up," she said happily. "It doesn't look like as much as I thought it would. Four items, though. Mr. and Mrs. Young have a new grandchild in Skowhegan, and Bart Temple is home on leave. The Grange is throwing a public supper the first week in December. And Archie Henson just got back from visiting his daughter in Vermont."

"That sounds like a nice variety," said Judith. When the children had washed and gathered around the table, she broke her own news to them.

"Joel is sick," she said calmly, though she was terrified. "His commanding officer wrote to tell us that he's in the infirmary. They'll let us know if there's any change."

"But we just heard from him yesterday, and he was fine," Bobby protested, his eyes growing round with confusion.

"It struck him suddenly." Judith reached over and patted Bobby's hand.

"Is it bad?" asked Ned.

"Well…I think it must be, or Joel would have written himself." She tried not to sound too pessimistic.

"Is it influenza?" Christina asked fearfully.

"Yes."

"Judith!" Christina's eyes flared with panic. "People are—"

"Hush," said Judith. "Joel is in God's hands. We must all pray hard for him." She asked the blessing, adding a petition for Joel's health.

Christina sat brooding during the meal, but Judith talked cheerfully to the children. She knew that if Bobby realized how dire Joel's situation was, he would become despondent again.

She had a private word with Christina as they washed the dishes. "We have to be careful not to let the children become too fearful and depressed. It's up to us to set the example."

"But, Judith, influenza! They say men are dropping like flies from it. They're dying! Mrs. Gardner is afraid she'll hear any day that Harry is dead."

"Don't, Christina! We have to hope and pray. It's a terrible disease all right, but more men recover than die." She emptied her dishpan and rinsed it out, then turned it upside down to drain in the cast iron sink. "I was thinking perhaps I should go down there to help nurse Joel. They must be short-handed."

"You can't!" Christina cried. "What would we do without you? First mother, then Joel, and now Father's gone. You can't!"

Judith sighed. "Pray hard, Christina."

There was a knock at the door.

"That will be Mr. Thayer," Christina said.

"Let me get it," Judith told her. "Go in the front room and get your news items ready. I just want to speak to him about Joel for a moment."

Christina left the kitchen meekly, and Judith took off her apron. She walked slowly to the door.

"Good evening, Judith." After a quick look at her face, Ben asked, "Is everything all right?"

"I hope so, Mr. Thayer. We've heard today that Joel is ill. Influenza. I wondered if I might consult with you later about it, after you've finished with Christina's business. I'm not sure what is the best thing for me to do, and I was hoping someone could advise me."

"Of course." He stepped inside and removed his hat.

Judith took it and his coat. "Christina is ready for you." She led him to the front room, where her parents always entertained company.

The kerosene lamp gleamed from the top of the desk. Christina had her papers spread out on the secretary, and had placed a second chair beside it for Ben. She rose to greet him when Judith ushered him in.

"I'll bring you some coffee," Judith said. She went to the kitchen, passing through the dining room, where the boys and Lydia were playing Parcheesi. She had instructed them to be quiet during Mr. Thayer's visit and promised a reward of turnovers. She fixed their treats first, with glasses of milk, and carried the tray to the dining room.

"You're being so good and quiet," she said, ruffling Bobby's hair. "As long as you behave, you can stay up and play your game until Mr. Thayer is gone."

She went back to the kitchen and poured coffee for Ben and herself, and milk for Christina. She filled a plate with turnovers and gingersnaps and carried the tray to the front room this time, where she set it on a side table and began unloading it.

"Thank you, Judith," Ben said, accepting his coffee cup from her. "Your sister has done a creditable job for her first day. I've only had a couple of minor changes to suggest." He took a sip from his cup.

Christina took her glass of milk and a raisin turnover and tried to nibble delicately without spilling crumbs down the front of her blouse.

Judith sat down on the sofa across the room from them. She wished fervently that her mother were there to guide her, because of the captain's letter about Joel. And because of Ben Thayer.

She lifted her gaze to his face, then looked down again. She blew on her coffee and took a sip. She couldn't speak. Every time she tried, the muscles in her throat seemed to constrict. And when she looked at Ben, his solemn blue eyes locked hers, seeming to try to extract from her the words she couldn't say.

She took a deep breath. "I'm glad Christina's efforts please you. Are you finished with the *Hummer's* business for tonight?"

"I think so," Ben smiled. "I've asked her to go on gathering news as she can through the week. She can drop it off anytime by Friday night, and on Saturday I'll lay out the second issue. This young lady is going to make a fine reporter."

Christina smiled, flushing at his praise.

Judith nodded. "Good. Christina, would you please let me have a few moments with Mr. Thayer? I'm going to explain Joel's situation, and perhaps he can help me see if there's anything we can do."

Christina got slowly to her feet. Judith supposed she wanted to stay and listen, but it would be hard enough speaking to Ben without her younger sister there, her large brown eyes filling with fear as they spoke of Joel's chances.

"Is it very bad?" Ben asked when Christina had gone, his voice full of concern.

Judith got up and took the letter from her skirt pocket.

"We don't really know." She handed it to him. "It's not very specific. Would you please tell me what you make of it?"

He nodded and took out the single sheet of paper, unfolded it, and scrutinized it in the lamplight. Judith went back to the sofa.

"Hmm. You're right, it's quite vague. He's ill, but it doesn't say how bad."

"He would have written himself if he could," Distress cracked Judith's voice.

"Probably." Ben was quiet. "Perhaps I could telephone this Captain LeMore tomorrow."

"On Sunday?" Judith was startled at the thought of driving to the store to use the telephone on Sunday. "The store won't be open."

He shrugged. "George will open up for me to use the telephone. You need more information about your brother."

"Yes," she said, frowning. "Do you think I ought to go to Lewiston?"

"Would that help Joel?"

"I don't know. Mrs. Gardner spoke of going to nurse Harry. I wonder if Joel is getting good care, and if they have enough nurses."

"Do you have nursing experience?" Ben asked.

"No, but—he's my brother. I love him very much."

"But the other children need you."

"Yes." She looked up at him anxiously. "You're a praying man, Mr. Thayer."

He said slowly, "Yes, Judith, I am. I'll pray for Joel. I have been, anyway, but I will pray about this."

"I could take the train on Monday," she said.

"Where would you stay?"

"I don't know. Perhaps I should ask Aunt Alla if she knows anyone down there." She looked toward the dining room doorway. She could hear Ned's voice raised heatedly, and Christina trying to soothe him.

"Let's see if I can't get some information from the Army post tomorrow," Ben said. "I'll go after church and see if I can get through to someone. They would know the situation better."

"Thank you, Mr. Thayer."

"Judith," he said, setting the coffee cup and saucer down on the secretary.

She brought her eyes slowly up to meet his gaze.

"Can't you call me Ben?"

She opened her mouth to say something, then closed it again and looked down at the rug. After a moment, she said, "It's so—" She shook her head in futility.

"Not afraid of me, are you?"

She made herself look at him and shake her head slightly, but it turned into a shrug. She stood quickly to hide her embarrassment and, looking at the tray of cookies, said, "Thank you for coming."

After a pause, he stood. "I'll see you at church in the morning, and then I'll go to the store and see what I can find out." He gathered Christina's papers.

"God promises us peace, but I can't seem to stop worrying," she confessed as she handed him his coat and hat.

"Trust Him," Ben said gently. "He will do what's best for your brother."

*****

In the morning, Ned spotted Uncle Henry and Aunt Alla Bickford driving into the church yard just ahead of them. Christina was driving the Chadbournes' wagon, with Chub in harness. When she pulled up, Judith instructed Ned to help Christina unhitch and secure the horse. She hurried across the churchyard to intercept her aunt.

"So Wesley is gone to Portsmouth?" was Aunt Alla's greeting, as she bent to kiss Judith on the cheek.

"Yes, he left Friday."

"You children must spend Thanksgiving with us."

"Thank you," said Judith. "What shall we bring?"

"A kettle of squash and a couple of pies?" her aunt asked.

"That's fine. Aunt Alla, Joel is sick. We had a letter from his captain yesterday."

"Oh, dear." She looked grave, and Uncle Henry turned to listen.

"Influenza?" he asked, unbuckling his horse's bridle.

Judith nodded.

Aunt Alla put her hand on Judith's arm. "We must pray."

"Auntie, do you think I should go down to Lewiston?" Judith asked. "Could I help Joel if I went?"

"I don't know, dear. You might just be in the way. And if you contracted the disease, where would that leave the children?" She shook her head.

"I wouldn't advise it," Uncle Henry said.

Judith sighed. "If I could just do something."

"Wait and pray," said her aunt.

"Keep us posted," said Uncle Henry. "If you need to go down, we'll keep the children, but I wouldn't rush into it."

Judith turned to make sure all of the Chadbournes entered the church together. Ben was walking toward her.

"I'm still planning to make that inquiry for you," he said quietly.

Judith nodded. "Thank you."

"I'll stop at your house on my way home."

She hustled Bobby and Lydia toward the church door somewhat comforted.

# Chapter 8

He came at twilight. Judith was in the barn, and Bobby guided Ben to her, where she sat on a stool milking Gwendoline.

"Hello, Judith." His eyes were warm in the lantern light. He leaned on the dividing wall between the stalls.

Christina, in the next stall milking Edith, looked under the red cow's belly and called, "Hello, Mr. Thayer."

"Hello, Scoop," he replied, and Christina laughed.

He bent toward Judith, and she kept up the rhythm of her milking, looking up at him, anxious to hear his news.

"I couldn't get Captain LeMore, but I did speak to someone at the infirmary."

"What did you find out?" Judith asked.

"Joel is very sick. Not critical, but serious."

"Should I—"

Ben shook his head. "Not yet, I think. The fellow said if I call tomorrow I can speak to the doctor. Let's do that. He'll be able to give me a better report. I'll ask him if he thinks you could help Joel's recovery. If he says yes, I'll inquire about lodging and so forth."

"Thank you." Gwendoline's milk was drying up, and she didn't give much that night. Judith stood up and moved the pail and her stool out of the stall. "I really appreciate your doing this," she said, moving past Ben. Bobby and Ned stood behind him, wide-eyed.

"Say, boys, how's school going?" Ben asked cheerfully.

"Fine, sir," said Ned.

"Good," said Bobby.

"Can you read, Bobby?" Ben asked.

"Yes, sir."

Ben's eyes widened. "Truly? You must be quite a scholar. What grade are you?"

"First," Bobby said with pride. "Judith helps me."

"I should have you come sort type for me, if you know all your letters."

"Can third-graders do that?" Ned asked hopefully.

"I don't see why not." Ben followed Judith to the threshing floor. "I'll print the *Hummer* in the morning and take it around to the post office and the store. I'll make the call when I get to the store, and I'll stop here on my way back, but I may be gone for a while. I plan to give this first issue to anyone who will take it."

"Just give it away?" Judith asked.

"Yes, so folks can see it. People like to get something for free. And once they see how good it is, they might want to buy an ad, or subscribe, or give Christina some news."

Judith shook her head. "I don't think I have much business sense. How many papers are you going to print?"

"Oh, I think I'll be optimistic with this first run and print a hundred. We'll see how many people come back for more next week."

Christina came in, carrying a lantern in one hand and her milk pail in the other. "Not much milk tonight," she said.

"No, they're all going dry," Judith agreed. "But Ethelwynn should calve before Christmas. I hope we'll have enough milk to drink until then."

"Say, Scoop," said Ben, "I put a box on page two of the first issue announcing your employment and recommending that people send their news to you. They can mail it or call on you. That all right?"

"Sure," Christina said with a grin. "I wish we had a telephone."

"Well, it may not be long now," Ben said. "Meanwhile, we'll get by. If we get a lot of subscriptions, I may have to hire some boys to deliver the papers, though." He reached inside his coat and brought out a folded sheet of paper. When he unfolded it, the girls saw that it was about a foot and a half long and three inches wide. "This is the banner. I made a sample and brought it along to show you."

He held it out, and Judith took one end. *Sidney Hummer*, it said in large Old English letters. At each side, a hummingbird silhouette faced the lettering. In smaller type, below a double line, it said, "Vol. I, No. 1, November 22, 1918." Like all of Ben's creations, it was flawless.

"Impressive," Christina breathed.

"Very nice," Judith agreed.

"Can't change it now." Ben chuckled and bent to pick up the two pails. "Ladies, if you would precede me with a lantern, I'll take these in for you."

Judith blew out the flame in the lantern they always left in the barn. Bobby and Ned ran ahead in the dark, then came Christina carrying the small lantern, then Ben with the milk pails, and Judith close behind him.

Ben turned his head to the side and said over his shoulder, "I don't suppose you'd like to ride along with me tomorrow?"

"I couldn't," said Judith. She had housework and laundry to do, besides going over her wardrobe in case she should be going to Lewiston. But even if that were not the case, she didn't think she could ride about town in Ben's buggy with him, opening herself to stares and speculation.

He accepted her refusal without comment and followed Christina carefully through the woodshed and into the kitchen at the back door. "They're bringing electric lines out here in the spring."

"I'll believe it when I see it," Christina said. "They have it on the main road, but they passed right by us. We'll probably be the last people in Maine to get it."

"Oh, no, I saw Mr. Tatum from the power company the other day, and he assured me I'll have service soon."

"Really? They can't get to your house without passing ours." Christina laughed. "Are you getting a telephone, too?"

"That's next on my list. Need it for the business."

So, it was definite, Judith thought. If Ben Thayer asked for electric power, they would get it. Her father had never pressed the issue, even though the lines came within half a mile of River

Rest. He always said it would be too expensive, and they could get along fine without it.

"Mr. Thayer," Ned said shyly, "did you mean it about having boys sort letters for you?"

Ben looked inquiringly at Judith, and she raised her shoulders just a little. "Well, I most certainly did. If your sister doesn't mind, I could use you after school Mondays. I'll be flinging type everywhere tomorrow morning. I'm coming by in the afternoon, and if you boys are home, I'll take you back with me for a while. It's worth a dime apiece."

"You don't have to," Judith said quickly.

Ben smiled at the bright-eyed boys. "My gain."

*****

The children were out the door, heading for school the next morning when Ned came running back inside.

"Judith! Mr. Thayer just left a paper for us!"

Judith took it from him and unfolded it with wonder. The *Hummer* was a reality. She stood on the doorstep looking at it, as the four children walked off toward the school a mile and a half away. She shivered. She would have to let Christina start taking the wagon to school soon, and when the snow came Chub would pull the sled.

She went inside and poured herself a cup of tea, deciding to steal ten minutes from her overloaded day. She had large pans of water heating on the wood stove for her washing, but it wasn't hot yet. She sat at the table in the dining room and read every word of the *Hummer*.

Ben's editorial on the end of the war and its probable impact on the community thrilled her. His writing was stirring, patriotic, but well-reasoned. The young men would return soon to put the energy they had given to the cause of freedom into their farms and their businesses. Families would be reunited, and the town would flourish.

She was surprised at the number of illustrations in the little paper. There were several ads for the *Hummer* itself and Ben's printing services, but also some for other businesses. Farmer Richard Blake was advertising Jersey breeding stock. The general store had a large ad, and the woolen mill in Oakland advertised a sale on blankets. Nearly every ad had an illustration of some sort, a cow for Blake's spot, a waterwheel for the woolen mill, and a balance scale for the store. Judith wondered if Ben had given free ads in the first issue.

A smattering of local news was also included. A few tidbits Ben had gleaned at the post office and the store the week before, she guessed. He had also written a feature on Thanksgiving. He had asked several of the town's best cooks what they would be serving on the holiday. It made for interesting reading. Christina could write stories like that, Judith thought. There were two cartoons and a half column of classified ads. "Place your ad here next week for 25 cents," said one.

When she had read every line, Judith started guiltily. Her ten minutes had stretched to twenty. She folded the paper carefully, set it on the secretary for Christina to read that afternoon, and gathered the dirty laundry into a large heap on the kitchen floor. Her labor hadn't lessened since her father had left. If anything, she had more to do now, and Joel's illness had her fretting, but she felt a grain of optimism that hadn't been there before. The *Hummer* had lifted her spirits. She hoped suddenly that it wouldn't fail, and that Ben's promise would be realized.

*****

Ben was back at the Chadbournes' at three thirty, with Lydia, Bobby, and Ned in his buggy.

"Hope you don't mind," he said when Judith went to the doorstep and looked questioningly at him. "I was passing the school at the right time, and thought I'd give them a ride. Christina's out gathering news."

"It's all right. Can you come in?"

He hid his surprise and jumped down from the buggy, tied Chester's reins to an iron ring in the granite hitching post, then followed her inside. The boys pounded up the stairs.

"Boys, change your clothes if you're going to help Mr. Thayer," Judith called after them. She turned to Ben. "Would you like some coffee?"

"No, I'd better not stop. I need to get home and build my fire up." He set a small paper sack on the dining room table. "That's for the children."

Judith stared at him in surprise. Slowly she picked up the bag and opened it. "Peanuts? Whatever for?"

He shrugged. "I thought it would give them something to think about besides the losses they've endured and your brother's condition."

"Thank you. I guess shelling these will take their minds off things for a few minutes. That and sorting type."

He smiled apologetically. "I'd have brought you something, but I don't think you're as easily distracted."

Fear leaped into her eyes. "Did you talk to the doctor?"

"Yes." He frowned, hating to bring her such bleak word, and reached to give her hand a comforting squeeze. "He says if you want to go down, it might be good for Joel. He'd get more attention that way. They have hundreds of sick men there, and not enough staff. There are boardinghouses where relatives stay, within walking distance." He grimaced as despair clouded her face. It wasn't what he'd hoped he could tell her. "I'm sorry, Judith."

She swallowed hard. "I'll speak to Aunt Alla. The children can go to her house for a few days. I'll take the train tomorrow."

"I'm making a business trip." It was out before he really thought about it. In watching her carefully, he could see she was straining to hold back tears, and it was imperative that he take some kind of action. "I could drive you down. In my car. I can get enough gasoline now."

"That's very kind, but—"

"I can have you there in two hours," he put in hastily, before she could outright reject the idea. "It would be more pleasant than the train, and it won't cost you anything."

"You just happen to have business in Lewiston?" She raised a skeptical eyebrow.

She hadn't said no, and Ben pressed his advantage. "Yes, well, there's a man I want to see there at the daily paper. I need to ask him some questions, take a sample of the *Hummer* down, and get some addresses for syndicates."

"You could get that from the editor in Waterville," said Judith.

"Yes, I could, but I don't want to. Listen, Judith, I can even take you down for the day. You can see Joel, spend several hours with him while I take care of business, and I can have you home by suppertime. Wouldn't that be better than you trying to find a place to stay and sending the children to your aunt's?"

She wavered, he could see it in her eyes. "If I can help Joel, I ought to stay there near him."

"Pack your things and be ready at seven in the morning. I'll take you down, and if he's feeling better, I'll bring you back home. If Joel really needs you, I'll help you find a boardinghouse."

"You would do all that, wouldn't you?"

He nodded, saying nothing.

When she opened her mouth, he knew she was about to refuse him courteously.

"Be ready," he said crisply. "I'll pick you up at seven."

The boys came tearing down the stairs, but halted and stood quietly beside her, with repressed excitement. Judith hesitated, and Ben decided he had won the skirmish. A quick retreat was in order.

"All set, fellows?"

"We sure are," Ned said.

"I'll need them home for chores," Judith stipulated.

"I'll see that they're back in an hour."

The boys ran before him to the buggy. When he'd untied Chester's reins and jumped up onto the seat, Ben looked back. She stood in the doorway, watching him uncertainly. He waved and slapped Chester with the reins before she could call out to change things.

*****

Judith watched Chester trot smartly up the gravel road. *Well, I guess I'm going to Lewiston tomorrow.*

She closed the door against the chilly air and began to pack her clothing and prepare food for the trip. She had never ridden in an automobile before. None of their extended family was wealthy enough to own one. It was exciting, but a little scary. The boys would pump her afterward for details of the ride and ask mechanical questions she had no idea how to answer. She would have to take note of everything Ben did on the trip so she could satisfy their curiosity.

When Ned and Bobby returned an hour later, their emotions were wound up as tight as clock springs.

"Mr. Thayer gave us horehound candy," Bobby told her, his eyes large. "Do you care, Judith?"

"Well, that depends. Did you eat so much you won't want your supper?"

"No, just two pieces."

She laughed. "I guess you're not thoroughly spoiled yet." She made a mental note to reserve the bag of peanuts for when they returned from Uncle Henry's.

"We helped Mr. Thayer do his chores," Ned said importantly.

"Good boys."

He shrugged. "It wasn't hard. He sold all his beef, and Chester's all alone in the barn now. It hardly took a minute to clean his stall and feed him. Bobby and I rubbed him down. Then we went up to the house and sorted type. That was the best part. He has alphabets in three different sizes."

"The letters are all backward, Judith!" Bobby's eyes shone with excitement.

Ned frowned at him. "Bobby did the biggest ones and I did the rest. We didn't finish, though."

"How come the boys get to do all the fun stuff and I had to stay home and churn?" Lydia grumbled.

Judith smiled in sympathy. "We've got to do our own chores up quickly tonight and pack a bag for each of you," she said, meeting the eyes of the three solemn children. "Mr. Thayer will take me to see Joel tomorrow, and if I don't come home by dark, you'll go to Aunt Alla and Uncle Henry's to stay overnight."

"Goody!" Lydia cried. "I can sleep in Molly's room!"

Judith smiled at her enthusiasm. The children always enjoyed spending time with their cousins. "Ned, can you run over there tonight with a message?"

"Sure."

She hesitated. It was cold, and would soon grow dark. "Maybe I'd better hitch Chub and drive over."

"Let me ride Lady," Ned begged. "I'll be back before you know it."

Lady was old and gentle. Judith decided Ned would be safe on her with Father's saddle for the mile-long ride. "All right, but hurry right back. If you're not back soon, I'll be worried."

When he had gone, she and Lydia and Bobby went to the barn. The milking was not tedious now, and Bobby shook down hay for all the animals. Lydia got the horses' rations, leaving Lady's in her feed box.

Christina and Ned came back together, riding double on Lady's broad back.

"Ned met me on the road," Christina called, jumping down outside the barn door. "Are you really going to see Joel tomorrow?"

"Yes, and you'll be in charge here," Judith replied.

Ned led Lady into her stall. "Aunt Alla says it's fine. Uncle Henry will drive over after supper, and if you're not home, he'll take us to their house."

"That's perfect," Judith said with relief. "You'll have time to do the chores. Christina, you'll have to come right home after school tomorrow. Be sure to bank the fires before you leave, if you go to Auntie's."

She and Christina were up late, packing everyone's bags and the children's lunches for school. She made up a parcel to take to Joel, and packed two days' worth of food for herself so she wouldn't have to buy much if she stayed.

"Would you take this to Harry?" Christina hesitantly held out a crumpled envelope.

Judith took it and put it in her handbag, trying not to stare at it. "I'm sure he's better by now."

"I—I hope so. But I wanted him to know we're thinking of him."

Judith nodded. "If I can see him, I'll tell him personally and give him your message. If not, I'll leave it with someone at the infirmary."

Christina nodded, tears glistening in her dark eyes. "How much will a boardinghouse cost?"

"I don't know." Judith took the rest of the money their father had left in her care—seven dollars and thirty cents—and packed it in her bag.

"Maybe Ben would give me an advance," Christina suggested.

"Don't even think it. He's doing too much already. I won't take money from him." Judith set her mouth determinedly as she closed her traveling bag. She remembered the fleeting touch of Ben's hand on hers. Commiseration in a sad moment, that was all. She mustn't read more into it. She would maintain a discreet distance from Ben, no matter how polite and helpful he made himself. And no matter how her heart melted when he spoke to her in tender sympathy.

# Chapter 9

Judith and Ben were seated in the captain's office at the army camp at ten o'clock Tuesday morning. The furnishings were meager and utilitarian in the building that had been part of a girls' academy, but the plaster work on the ceiling was gorgeous, and an ornate marble fireplace dominated one end of the room.

"I'm sorry, Miss Chadbourne, I wish I could have reached you," said Captain LeMore. "I'd have saved you the trip."

"My brother—" Judith said faintly.

"Is being sent home soon," LeMore said.

"Home?" Judith looked at him blankly.

"Yes. The decision was made this morning. His unit is being disbanded."

Judith sank back in her chair, limp after hours of anxiety.

The captain continued, "Your brother's unit was hit hard. Sixty percent of the men contracted influenza. We'll be discharging those who are ill. The healthy ones will fill the ranks of other units that have lost men to the epidemic."

"Joel is coming home—when?" she asked.

"We'll evaluate each case. When the doctor feels they're past the contagious stage and able to travel, they'll be sent home. The doctor can answer your questions."

"May I see Joel?"

LeMore hesitated. "I hate to send healthy civilians into the infirmary. It might be better for you to wait until he comes home. We'll send him on the train—"

Judith set her jaw. "I want to see my brother."

Ben sat forward. "Captain, I'll escort Miss Chadbourne. She's been very concerned for her brother, and she's traveled a long way. A short visit…"

LeMore sighed and stood up. "All right. I don't recommend it, but if you insist … Just go to the front door of the infirmary and ask for Private Chadbourne."

"I've brought him some food," said Judith. "May I take it to him?"

"Dr. Berrick is the man you want to talk to. He can tell you if your brother is able to eat solid food. He can also give you a better idea of when he'll be discharged."

"Come, Judith," said Ben.

"Wait. I wanted to ask about Harry Gardner." She turned back to the captain. "Private Gardner's family are neighbors of ours. We've been praying for Harry. He's a dear friend of my brother's, and I wondered if I could see him as well."

The captain consulted some papers on his desk.

"I'm sorry," he said slowly. "We sent a telegram this morning. Private Gardner died just after midnight."

*****

When they were on the sidewalk, Judith turned to Ben. "You don't need to go inside with me. Just go see that editor and come back for me later."

"I'm not leaving you alone," Ben said.

"You might be exposed to influenza."

He said nothing, but walked steadily with her to the Oldsmobile and retrieved from the back seat the basket she had filled for Joel.

"I'm sorry about the Gardner boy," he said.

Judith swallowed hard, blinking back the tears. Joel mustn't see her crying.

The orderly inside the infirmary door showed them to one of the many wards, where twenty men lay on beds. Beneath each iron cot lay a rifle and a bag of the occupant's belongings. Some of the ill men slept, while others moaned and tossed. A few looked more or less alert. One read a newspaper, and another had a Bible open on the blanket.

- 81 -

"Joel!" Judith ran to the bedside when she spotted her brother. He opened his eyes and slowly smiled.

"Judith." It was a faint whisper.

She tried not to show how shocked she was by his gaunt face. "Are you all right? How silly of me! Of course you're not." She brushed tears from her cheek with the back of her hand, angry with herself for not being able to control her emotion.

Ben produced a chair from somewhere, and she sat down, holding Joel's hand. She couldn't bear to think how he must have looked a couple of days ago.

"Ben." Joel looked past his sister in surprise. "You brought Judith?"

"Yes. I'm glad to be able to see you for myself."

"Christina's working for Ben now, writing for his newspaper," Judith told him.

"Really?" Joel's weary eyes seemed to light up a little.

"I brought you a copy." Ben laid a folded copy of the *Hummer* beside Joel.

"Thanks," said Joel. "I'll try to read it soon."

"Don't rush it," Ben recommended. "Just get strong, and you'll be coming back home."

"That's what the doc said this morning," Joel agreed.

"Can you eat cookies?" Judith asked. "I brought you some cookies and rolls and apples."

"Good. They haven't been feeding me very well. Of course, I couldn't hold it down for a while there."

"You're better now," Judith said.

"Yes."

She talked to him quietly, giving him all the news from home. Ben stood by patiently, answering the occasional question Joel threw his way. After half an hour, the boy's eyes were drooping.

Judith leaned forward to brush the hair back from his forehead. "We'd better let you rest."

"I'll be home soon," he said feebly.

"Yes, dear. We'll coddle you something fierce."

- 82 -

Joel tugged at the blanket and turned on his side. "I wonder how Harry's doing."

Judith darted a glance at Ben. He put his hand out, touching her lightly on the shoulder. Tears filled her eyes as she gazed up at him. He seemed to understand her silent plea, and he nodded slightly.

She stood up. "I'm going to let Ben sit with you for a moment, while I check with Dr. Berrick on your release."

Joel blinked. "All right. Will you ask him about Harry?"

Judith turned away and stepped quickly toward the door of the ward.

*****

Ben watched Judith leave the ward and then sat down in the chair.

"Joel, you need to get your strength back." He watched the face that was thinner and more lined than it should have been on a nineteen-year-old boy. He wasn't sure it was good to tell an invalid his best friend had died, but he felt that Joel would see withholding the news as a betrayal. He would fret over Harry's fate if he didn't know, and might blame him and Judith later for not telling him.

"I asked the doctor about Harry this morning, but he never came back and told me." Joel's eyes were glazed, and Ben put his hand to the boy's forehead, but he didn't seem to have a fever.

He sent up a quick prayer and made a decision. Leaning forward, he said softly, "This is going to be a blow, Joel. I'm not sure I should tell you, but I can see it's worrying you. Harry didn't make it."

Joel blinked twice and turned his face away.

Ben waited as the boy took several ragged breaths.

Joel turned back to look at him. "Does Judith know?"

"Yes. The captain told us just before we came over here."

Joel nodded. "The doc says I'll get better, though."

"Yes, you most certainly will. You're past the crisis, my friend. Your family needs you badly, so you need to do everything you can to regain your health."

Joel bit his cracked, peeling lip and nodded. "Is Pa all right?"

"Yes, he's fine. I asked your sister on the way down, and he's doing well at the shipyard. He'll try to come home for Christmas. It's going to be all right, Joel. Your family will be together again."

"I didn't do anything to help with the war." His disappointment was obvious, and Ben reached out to squeeze his forearm. "You were willing. You and Harry both. If the timing had been different, you'd have been out there with the best of them."

"I didn't want to come," Joel confessed.

"Of course not. You had a family to think about. Your father was ill for a time. But he's better now, Joel."

"Are you sure?"

"Yes. I spoke to him the day before he left for Portsmouth. He misses your mother something terrible, I think, but … " He shook his head, knowing how deep and debilitating a man's sorrow could be. "He'll come through for the kids, Joel."

Joel swallowed. "I will, too."

Ben nodded. "Let me get you a drink of water."

He held Joel up to drink, then made him as comfortable as he could. The boy's eyelids drooped again.

"Thanks for coming, Ben. And thanks for telling me."

Ben grasped his hand for an instant. "It's all right. Just get better and come home."

He found Judith in the entry, speaking to Dr. Berrick. Her eyes widened in a question when she saw him.

"I told him," Ben said shortly. "He'll be all right."

"Chadbourne's a strong lad," the doctor said. "I expect he'll be leaving us soon."

"When?" Judith pressed.

"After Thanksgiving, but within a week, probably, unless he has a relapse."

"Does that happen often?" Judith quavered.

"No, most of them turn a corner and start to mend. It can take a while. We'll send you a wire when he's discharged, so you can meet his train. When he comes home, he'll need a lot of rest."

"We'll baby him," Judith said.

Ben had his own thoughts on the subject. He knew Joel wouldn't want to be babied. He would want to be useful, rather than feel he was a drag on his family. But there was time enough to get that concept across to Judith.

*****

On the doctor's orders, they washed their hands before they went out to Ben's car. Judith's heart felt lighter than it had in days. Joel was well enough that she could go home to the children.

"I don't know how to thank you."

"I was glad to do it." Ben opened the door for her on the passenger side, then went around and climbed into the driver's seat.

"I wasn't sure we ought to tell him about Harry, but he seemed so worried," Judith said.

"He needed to know." Ben drove to the newspaper office and invited Judith to go in with him.

"I'll just be in the way," she said.

"No, it's too cold out here. Please come in."

She gave in and went into the office with him. The editor, Daniel Williams, greeted Ben enthusiastically and scanned the *Hummer* as Judith and Ben stood by.

"Not bad," Williams said appreciatively. "Not bad for a first issue."

"A little thin," Ben said.

"You have some nice features. Lots of art. It's attractive. Think you can make a go of it?"

"I've got to," Ben smiled. "I've promised this young lady the *Hummer* will turn a profit within a year."

"Oho," said Williams, looking at Judith over his spectacles, and she found herself blushing.

Ben and Williams talked for half an hour, and Judith listened with interest, looking about at the office and watching workers come and go.

Ben stood at last and held out his hand to Williams. "Thank you for the tips, sir. If you're ever in Sidney…"

Williams laughed. "If I am, it will be because I'm lost. But stay in touch, Thayer. I'll be interested to see what your paper develops into."

When they got out to the sidewalk, Ben asked, "Are you hungry?"

"I brought enough food to last me a couple of days if I stayed," Judith laughed. "If you feel like a picnic…"

"It's a little cold for that," Ben said. "I think there's a restaurant up the street."

"No, don't do that," Judith cried. Restaurants were expensive establishments her family avoided. "Just find a place to stop. We can eat in the car. I promise you, I won't drop any crumbs. And I have a bottle of sweet cider."

He eyed her closely, and Judith was afraid he would insist that they eat in town. He probably thought that would be pleasant, but she would feel guilty if he spent money on her, and she wasn't sure she could eat with strangers all about, staring at them.

He smiled. "All right, let's head out. We can find a place to stop and eat when we get outside town." He guided her back to his car and opened the door for her.

"I really think Joel will be fine, don't you?" she asked anxiously as he got in.

"Yes, I do. He's got a good constitution."

Judith took a deep breath and tried not to look at Ben too much. It was unnerving when he looked over at her with those deep, compassionate eyes. She stared ahead, out the windshield. On the way down, they had been quiet. Ben had spoken to her a few times, and she had answered him, but her nerves had kept her from engaging in real conversation. The smooth movement of the automobile had surprised her, and it had taken only minutes for her to forget her initial fear of riding in the machine, but her anxiety for her brother and feelings of awkwardness had kept her quiet.

She felt more at ease with Ben now, but was still a little in awe of him. Ben's confidence in Joel's recovery went a long way toward alleviating her worry.

But now other thoughts crowded her mind, not the least of which was Ben's generosity. A few short weeks ago, she had seen him as a sinister presence in her life. His meddling had felt threatening. Now his presence was a bulwark. That didn't seem right. She was supposed to depend on her family, not a man she hardly knew.

"I don't know what I'd have done without you today," she ventured. "I mean, if I came down alone on the train."

"I'm glad I could be of service." He kept his eyes on the road, but the sincerity in his voice could not be doubted.

Judith sat back and willed herself to relax. One couldn't stay wound up tight all day. She watched the city fade away, surprised at the number of automobiles they met, though they were far outnumbered by farm wagons and buggies.

The road was well maintained within the town limits, but deteriorated as they went into the countryside. Ben drove slowly, avoiding ruts and potholes in the gravel road. Judith watched his movements carefully and tried to memorize the interior of the Oldsmobile sedan. She even asked him a few questions, ones she thought Ned would ask her later.

Half an hour out of town, he pulled over where a farm lane meandered off toward a field of corn stubble. He brought Judith's food basket over the back of the seat, and they enjoyed an impromptu lunch of sandwiches, apples, carrots, pickles, and cookies. When Judith had packed up the remains, Ben once more turned the auto into the road.

She was definitely feeling more at ease with him. They talked quietly of commonplace things: her family, the *Hummer*, farm work.

"Why did you decide to buy a farm?" Judith was emboldened to ask.

"Why wouldn't I?"

"I've wondered," she admitted. "A city man like you."

He laughed. "Me? I'm not a city man."

"But you lived in New York—"

"For a while. I was born on a farm north of Albany. My father sent me to New York to study art."

She thought about that. "It must have been quite a sacrifice for your family."

"I suppose it was. But my older brother was married and helping my father with the farm. My sisters all settled nearby. My parents could tell that farming wasn't my great passion, I guess. They managed to send me to college. I took a year in Albany, but I really wanted a chance to study art."

"It seems so exotic," Judith said.

He smiled. "New York, the evil city. It is, in some ways."

"You wound up in publishing."

"Well, I found a part time job with a printer to finance my art lessons. Then I worked a stint on a newspaper, and went into an advertising house for a couple of years, drawing illustrations for ads."

She thought of the illustrated ads in the *Hummer*. "You were good at it."

He smiled. "I did all right. Caught the eye of the art director at *Uptown New York*. He took me on and taught me a lot before he retired. Next thing I knew, I had his job."

They were on the outskirts of Augusta, and had just ten miles to go. The afternoon was waning.

"Why did you give it up?" she asked softly.

He didn't answer for several seconds, then he sighed. "I'd had enough, that's all."

But Judith felt somehow that wasn't all.

"I bought an automobile and decided to just drive wherever the road took me." He threw a sideways glance at her. "I suppose I could have gone Out West."

"Or back to northern New York?"

"I wasn't ready to be back there," he said, and she knew there was more he wasn't telling her. "I drove all day and stopped that night in Sturbridge, Massachusetts. I didn't have a map. I just picked a road that looked like it led to nowhere."

"Sidney, Maine?"

He laughed. "No, the next thing I knew, I was pointed toward Boston. Had to do something about that. I detoured north and wound up in New Hampshire. The third day, I crossed into Maine, and I finally felt like I was ready to stop driving. I started looking for a quiet place."

"That's why you bought the Drakes' house. For peace and quiet."

"Yes. I drove and drove and drove, and I got off on this awful little road in a town that wasn't even a hamlet, just farms spread all over. And then I came by a house that had a For Sale sign stuck in the yard. I drove up the driveway and looked around. Snug little house with a tight barn. Splendid view of the Kennebec. Birds and buttercups and a woodlot."

"I guess the Drakes were glad to see you coming," said Judith. "They were anxious to sell and move to Islesboro to be near their daughter."

"They didn't argue when I brought out four thousand dollars in cash."

Her eyes widened. "Heavens."

"Yes, I was carrying everything I owned with me."

"Not a printing press."

He laughed. "No, I bought that a couple of months later. Rode the train to Portland to see a friend. My old boss from the magazine. He asked me to meet him at the *Telegram* office."

"He wanted you to go back to New York," Judith speculated.

"It did enter the conversation." Ben turned onto River Road, and Judith felt she was back in her own environment. "I told him I was done with the city, and we settled an arrangement where I'd mail him a few drawings now and then. And I bought a nearly obsolete printing press the Portland paper was done with."

"And Thayer's print shop, Sidney, Maine was born," she concluded.

"Yes. And I've talked so long there's no time for me to learn about *your* fascinating youth."

Judith chuckled. "You know it all. I was born here. I took a year at the normal school and taught one year in Readfield. Our ride today is the farthest I've ever been from home."

"Really?"

"Yes. I owe you a vast debt for broadening my horizons."

He laughed, and she thought he wasn't nearly as formidable as he had seemed a month earlier. Did she dare to think of him as a friend?

He pulled into the driveway of the farmhouse at twilight, and her siblings poured out the door, shouting with excitement. Ben unloaded her bags as she gave the clamoring children a report on Joel.

She turned to face him, feeling anything she said would be inadequate. It came out simply, "Thank you, Mr. Thayer."

He looked long and deeply into her eyes. "Ben," he said quietly.

She swallowed.

"I'll take you to the train when Joel comes," he said. "Let me know."

She nodded.

He turned and looked at Christina. "How's business, Scoop?"

"I couldn't do anything today—"

"I know. Take Thursday off for Thanksgiving, too. I'll have some news of our Army boys to write up myself. If you have anything tomorrow, bring it to me. Otherwise, I'll see you Friday."

He got into the car and drove slowly up the road.

Christina hung back as the other children went inside.

"Did you see Harry?"

A lump of sorrow formed in Judith's throat, and she shook her head. "Help me carry my things upstairs. We need to talk."

*****

Uncle Henry came an hour later, expecting to take four children home with him.

"Alla will be so disappointed if I come home alone," he said, when he found Judith had returned. "Let me take two or three, at least."

"They have to be at school in the morning, Uncle Henry," Judith protested.

"I'll drive them."

"Please, Judith?" Ned wheedled.

"I want to go," said Lydia. "I'm all packed."

"Let me take the young ones," their uncle said. "We'll keep them until you come for dinner on Thursday."

At last Judith relented.

"How about you, Bobby?" Uncle Henry asked.

Bobby shrank against Judith, shaking his head.

She put her arms around his shoulders. "I think Bobby will stay here with Christina and me."

"All right. Get your bags, kids, let's go!" Uncle Henry roared happily, and Lydia and Ned ran for their luggage.

# Chapter 10

A letter arrived from Portsmouth the next day. Judith's gratitude soared as she read her father's firm handwriting. His job was going well, and he was comfortably situated in a boardinghouse. He would try to send some money next week, and they could count on seeing him at Christmas.

Judith wrote to him that afternoon and told him Joel was coming home within a week. She briefly described her visit to the Army camp in Lewiston, and said Mr. Thayer had kindly given her a ride, as he had business in the city. She wished her father a happy Thanksgiving, and told him they all would miss him and pray for him.

She sighed, looking out the window, past the pasture to the river. She ought to tell Father about Christina's job. Instead, she signed off cheerfully and addressed the envelope. Time to peel the squash and bake the pies for the Thanksgiving feast at Uncle Henry and Aunt Alla's.

Christina had driven the wagon to school that morning. She dropped Bobby at home afterward.

"I'll take Lydia and Ned back to Aunt Alla's," she said to Judith.

Judith stood beside the wagon in the driveway, eyeing the children anxiously. "Do you need anything? Got plenty of clothes?"

"We're fine," Ned said.

She nodded. "Tell Aunt Alla I heard from Pa today, and he sounds well."

"I've got to get going if I'm going to get any news before dark," Christina said.

Judith waved as the horse jogged toward the road.

"See you tomorrow," Lydia called, waving.

Judith kept Bobby in the kitchen with her while she prepared supper and finished her baking for the family dinner the next day. Hector and Maude Sutton, from the Town Farm Road, came by in their wagon before sunset, and Judith went out to greet them, wiping her hands on her apron.

"Good afternoon. Won't you come in?"

"No, child, this is just a dooryard call," Mrs. Sutton said from her seat on the wagon box. "Hector's hankering for some yellow eye beans. Don't know why kidney and sulfur aren't good enough, but that's what he wants."

"We have some," Judith assured her, darting a glance at Hector. He was bundled up in a woolen coat and muffler, and his gray cap had ear flaps that tied under his chin, but she would recognize droll Mr. Sutton's laughing eyes anywhere.

"Figured you would," he boomed. "Your mother always planted yellow eyes."

"There, now, Hec," his wife said gently, her beady eyes watching Judith.

"How many would you like?"

"A couple of pounds," Mrs. Sutton said.

"Make it five," said her husband.

Judith went to the piazza. Bobby had already fetched a paper sack, and she quickly measured out the beans, weighing them on her mother's scale. It felt strange to be doing it. Was this what happened after a death? The same life went on, but different people performed the rituals?

"There you go," she said, handing the sack up to Mrs. Sutton. Hector reached across his wife and slipped fifty cents into her hand.

"You children all right without the folks?" he asked gruffly.

"Yes, sir."

"Wesley's gone to Portsmouth," Maude said flatly.

"Yes, ma'am. He'll be home for Christmas."

"And your brother?"

"He'll be home soon."

"That right?" Hector asked, his eyebrows shooting up.

- 93 -

"Yes, sir. He's been ill, but … they say he'll be able to come home soon."

"Too bad about Harry Gardner," said Maude.

Judith swallowed.

"Yes, his folks are worried sick about that boy," said Hector.

Judith realized the news of Harry's death hadn't reached the neighbors yet, but she was not going to be the one to break it. She had told no one but Christina, and had sworn her to silence, at least until they were certain the family had been informed.

"Thank you for inquiring." She dropped the two quarters into her skirt pocket as Hector lifted the reins. His brown gelding leaned into the collar and stepped out.

At five o'clock Christina was not home, and Judith started to fret. She and Bobby bundled up and went to the barn. They had finished the chores by lantern light and returned to the warm kitchen before she heard Christina drive Lady into the barn.

"Where were you?" she asked sharply, when Christina at last came in the back door.

"Getting news. I'm sorry. I didn't intend to be so late."

"I was worried." Judith took the pot of overdone green beans to the sink to drain it.

"Mrs. Perkins was giving me a lot of information about all the turkeys they've sold, and I stopped to give Mr. Thayer my news and ask him how long an article I should write about the turkeys."

Judith sighed. "You know I don't like you going there alone, especially after dark."

"Judith, you worry too much. I was there maybe ten minutes."

"You went in the house?" she asked anxiously.

"No, we stood on the piazza, and Ben gave me some pointers. It's going to be my first full-length article."

"Ben? You're calling him Ben?" Judith couldn't believe it. She herself strangled over the name.

"Not to his face," Christina conceded.

"Well, then, you should refer to him as Mr. Thayer."

"What are you so touchy about?"

Judith sighed. "Nothing. I was worried, that's all. I have to keep track of you children, and sometimes I'm not sure what to do."

"I'm sorry. I'll try to get home earlier next time. Maybe I can go out tomorrow morning for a little while."

"I don't want you to bother people on Thanksgiving."

"But I heard Dolly Burton's cousin is here for the holiday. You know, the mathematics professor. I thought maybe I could interview him. Find out what it's like to teach advanced mathematics."

"You hate mathematics."

"I know. But there must be something interesting about it."

Judith shook her head. "If you can write an interesting story about math, I'll know you're a true reporter."

Christina hesitated, then said quietly, "I stopped in at the Gardners', just for a minute."

Judith bit her upper lip and waited.

"They got the telegram this morning."

"I'm sorry." She set down the dish of beans and pulled Christina toward her. "I'm so sorry."

A little sob escaped Christina. "His mother said ..."

"What, dear?"

"He asked about me in his letters. He never wrote to me, you know, but he did ask about me."

Judith held her close. "I'm sure he asked Joel about you, too."

\*\*\*\*\*

The family spent a leisurely holiday at Aunt Alla and Uncle Henry's. Judith enjoyed seeing her cousins, and Uncle Frank and Aunt Sarah Chadbourne. She was able to relax, although she didn't sit still all morning. She kept busy, helping her aunts in the kitchen. The cousins had a noisy round robin going at the checkerboard in the parlor, with several spectators trying to give advice and others claiming the right to play the winner.

"Uncle Peter should be here," Aunt Alla lamented as Uncle Henry carved the turkey.

"He'd be here if he wanted to," said her husband.

"All you can do is invite him," Uncle Frank agreed. "He's chosen to live alone now. If you want to see him, you have to go where he is."

"I worry about him." Alla took a large spoonful of squash and passed the dish to her sister-in-law.

"I do, too," said Sarah. "I wonder if he's warm enough in that cabin."

After losing the family farm, Uncle Peter had retreated to a small house deep in the woods on Frank's property. He seldom left the acre Frank had deeded to him. Frank and Wesley and their sister Alla, with their spouses, made sure Uncle Peter's basic needs were met.

"He's too ashamed to show his face," Henry said. "I went up there last week to check on him, and he's got a decent woodpile. He'll be all right."

"But he doesn't have anyone to talk to," Alla persisted.

"That's the way he wants it," said her brother Frank.

"I'm making him a quilt," said Sarah. "Want to help me tie it, Alla?"

"Surely. How about tomorrow?"

"Wonderful. Judith, why don't you join us? Come over to my house, and we'll finish the quilt, and we can take it up to Uncle Peter when we take his supplies."

Judith accepted the invitation, although it meant taking another day off from her housework. She hadn't spent much time with her aunts since her mother's death, and she was longing for their companionship. She felt she'd been floundering in her new responsibilities as head of the household, and spending time with other adult women would help her gain confidence.

She asked Christina to drive her, Bobby, and Lydia to Aunt Sarah's house in the morning. Judith was glad Ned had decided to ride around in the wagon with Christina. Her brother's presence might add at least a modicum of respectability to Christina's news gathering.

"Just remember," she cautioned before going into Aunt Sarah's, "you two are out to get news, not to give it."

Ned laughed, but Christina nodded soberly and lifted the reins, clucking to Chub.

Two neighbor women, Maude Sutton and old Sadie Grafton, joined them for the quilting, and Judith's cousin, Lila Chadbourne, worked with them. For two hours the ladies worked at stitching the layers of the quilt together, with the talk flying as fast as the needles. Judith thought perhaps Christina should have stayed there to gather news. She jotted down a couple of especially noteworthy items to tell her sister. Christina might want to follow up on them for articles.

When the subject of Harry Gardner's death came up, Judith kept quiet. She didn't want to sensationalize it any more by revealing that she had known since Tuesday, but kept silent as Mrs. Sutton told the tale. Judith thought it was told with a bit too much relish. She grieved for the Gardner family. Harry was such a bright spot in all their lives. Everyone who knew him would miss him.

She had heard Christina weeping in the night after her trip to Lewiston, so hard that Judith was afraid Lydia would wake up. She'd gone in and sat on the bed, and Christina had cried harder, but no words had passed between them. Judith had put her arms around her and held her until the sobs subsided, then brought her a cool washcloth to wipe her face. "I'm so sorry, dear," she had whispered. Again this morning, Christina had come down to help with the chores with puffy, bloodshot eyes, and Judith knew she had shed more tears for Harry.

"And how's your brother?" Mrs. Sutton asked.

Judith's attention snapped back to the quilting bee. "Joel has been ill, but he's recovering now. The doctor tells me he'll be coming home soon."

"I'll worry about him until he gets out of that infirmary," Aunt Sarah said, shaking her head. "They say more soldiers die of disease than wounds."

"I saw him Tuesday," Judith said. "He was weak, but he had no fever. The doctor was very optimistic."

"Still," said Mrs. Sutton. "You'll have to watch him, make sure he doesn't overdo it. These men always want to be up and at it too soon."

"Yes, he could have a relapse," put in Sadie Grafton.

"Harry was a strong boy, too," Aunt Alla said fretfully.

Judith pressed her lips together and stitched on in silence.

"You went all the way to Lewiston, and back the same day?" Mrs. Sutton asked.

"Yes." Judith felt a flush creeping up to her cheeks.

"An exhausting trip on the train," the neighbor probed.

"She went by automobile," Aunt Alla said calmly.

Judith jumped up. "Can I start the potatoes for you, Aunt Sarah?" She didn't think she could bear it if one of her aunts let fall that Ben Thayer had driven her.

"Dear me, yes, it's half past eleven! Frank will be in for his dinner before I know it." Sarah stuck her needle into the cloth and rose. In the kitchen, Judith helped her put the vegetables on to cook and took the ironstone plates from the cupboard.

Lila came in from the dining room. "Mrs. Grafton and Mrs. Sutton are getting their coats on, Mama."

"I must see my neighbors off," Sarah said. "Lila, you get the milk and a jar of golden glow pickles. Judith, would you call Lydia and Janie down to set the table?"

Judith went to the stairway and called her sister's name. Lydia, Bobby and their cousin Janie, Sarah and Frank's youngest, came quickly down to the dining room.

Her aunts saw the neighbors to the door, and Judith heard their hearty good-byes and Sarah's thanks for their help. When the door closed behind them, it seemed very quiet, although the children bantered as they worked. Judith drew a deep sigh. She didn't *think* Ben's name had been mentioned.

Aunt Sarah handed her the butter dish. "Set that on the table, dear. Don't worry, now. Neighborhood news is one thing, but I won't let tales go round about my nieces."

The blush bloomed again on Judith's cheeks.

"There, now." Aunt Sarah smiled as Aunt Alla joined them. "Mr. Thayer's been a good neighbor."

"Yes," Judith managed. "He's a gentleman, Aunt Sarah."

"I'm sure of it." Sarah took a platter from her china closet.

Judith felt her aunt was reading something into the incident, although she was protecting her from the neighbors' speculation.

"There's nothing—I mean, he's so much older, Aunt Sarah. You don't think—"

"I don't think anything, dear. But Alla and I are here if you need advice at any time."

Judith turned in confusion toward Aunt Alla. She knew her cheeks were flaming, and Lila, four years her junior, seemed to be listening eagerly, though she didn't meet Judith's eyes directly.

"Auntie, I've been very careful."

"Of course you have," Alla said placidly. "And he's not so very old."

"Handsome," Sarah said. Her back was to Judith as she lifted the pot roast onto the platter.

Judith looked from one aunt to the other. Exasperated, she took the butter dish into the dining room and set it on the table.

"Are you all right, Judith?" Lydia asked, eyeing her as she laid out the napkins.

"I'm fine," Judith replied. "It's warm in the kitchen."

*****

After lunch, Judith and her aunts and Lila went back to work on the quilt. Lydia and Janie decided they wanted to learn how to tie the tufts of thread that held the layers together, and by two o'clock it was done.

"I must go," Alla declared. "I left Henry and Molly and the boys to fend for themselves this noon, so I must put a decent supper on the table."

Uncle Frank was loading his wagon with supplies for Uncle Peter. His two big Belgian horses stood patiently in harness.

"I thought we'd wait and take those things to him tomorrow," Sarah frowned, as Aunt Alla's buggy left the yard.

"I don't like the way the clouds are piling up," Frank replied. "We may be in for a snowstorm. I want to get these things to him today, just in case."

"You were working on the chicken coop," Sarah objected. "If it's going to snow, you need to finish that." She looked toward her niece. "Come with me, Judith. We can run the quilt and food to Peter, and your Uncle Frank won't have to leave what he was doing. Lila can watch the children."

Judith hesitated only an instant. Her extended family didn't call on her often, but when they did, she felt bound to respond, as she knew her mother would.

She rode in the wagon with her aunt, down the farm lane that crossed the pasture and over the rough woods road beyond.

"It's not a mile," Sarah told her, holding the reins firmly with her gloved hands, "but it seems like twenty."

Judith smelled the smoke from Uncle Peter's chimney first, and saw the little cabin when they emerged from the woods into his clearing. The horses stopped of their own accord before the door, and she and her aunt climbed down from the wagon. Judith took the new quilt and a basket of dry beans and coffee from the back of the wagon. Sarah hefted a box of baked goods and eggs as Judith stepped up to the door and knocked.

It was a long time before Uncle Peter opened the door, moving very slowly. His ashen skin was stretched tight over his face above his white beard.

"Who is it?" he asked feebly, blinking at Judith.

"I'm Judith," she replied.

"Wesley's oldest gal, Uncle Peter," Sarah said, pushing forward with her burden. "We brought you some grub and a quilt. Are you going to let us in?"

"It's a bare possibility." His voice was thin and reedy. He stepped aside and swung the door wider.

Judith followed Sarah in and set her basket on a rickety little table. She had been to his cabin only once before. It was as cramped and disorderly as she remembered it. Books, dishes, clothing and tools cluttered every surface.

Peter sank into his favorite rocking chair near the stove.

"Here," said Sarah, taking the quilt from Judith's arms. "This will keep you nice and snug this winter. Do you like it?"

Peter blinked at the quilt, his eyes traveling up and down its length. "It'll do," he grunted.

Uncle Peter used to come out of the woods on Thanksgiving and Christmas, and sometimes on Pa's or Uncle Frank's birthday. Judith realized with a shock that she hadn't seen him in three years. He seemed smaller and thinner. He was bald on top, but his fringe of white hair grew long in the back.

"That green piece there is from your mother's old apron," Sarah said, touching a small triangular patch. "You remember that apron?"

Peter nodded and ran a finger over the stitching.

"This yellow's a scrap from Janie's new school dress." Sarah gathered up the quilt and laid it folded across the foot of his rumpled bed. "So, how've you been?"

"Oh, I've been poorly these few weeks," he said.

"Have you, now?" Sarah frowned at him critically. "Been eating right?"

"I can't eat them beans anymore," he said fitfully. "Take 'em back with you."

"Take them back?" Sarah asked. Judith was startled at her offended tone. "Now, Peter, you need to eat."

"I don't feel like eating much," he confessed.

"What did you eat today?" Sarah crossed the room and lifted the lid of the pan on the stove. "What's that culch?"

"Soup," Peter said, not looking at her.

"My heavens, you're starving to death!" Sarah began pulling boxes and tins off his larder shelves and peering into them. Judith watched in amazement as Peter sat meekly ignoring the way his nephew's wife bullied him.

"Uncle Peter, you have plenty of food here," Sarah said at last. "Why aren't you eating it?"

"I had a flapjack yestiddy."

"A flapjack," Sarah snorted. "Judith, go get that box with the jar of stew from the wagon."

Judith hurried to obey, stepping out into the chilly wind. Darkness seemed to be falling early. She hoisted the last box from the wagon bed and took it inside.

"Here, now." Sarah lifted a Mason jar from the box. "This is good turkey stew Alla made from the leftover turkey last night. I'm putting it on to heat. You have that for your supper, you hear me?"

Peter nodded. "Just a mite."

Sarah shook her head in frustration. "I don't know why we let you stay up here by yourself. You're a stubborn old man."

Uncle Peter laughed, catching Judith's eye. "She says I'm stubborn."

Judith couldn't help smiling. "I guess it runs in the family."

"Yes," Sarah admitted. "I guess it does." She opened the stove and put two sticks in the firebox. "Judith, there's a woodpile outside against the wall. Just fill that woodbox, will you, now?"

Judith made several trips outside, trying not to keep the door open any longer than necessary. Every time she crossed the threshold, the change in temperature and smells struck her. Outside it was crisp and fresh. The air almost hurt her when she gulped big, piney breaths. Inside it was warm, too warm, really, and it smelled of kerosene, tallow, unwashed clothing, and Aunt Alla's turkey stew.

By the time she had finished, Aunt Sarah had Uncle Peter sipping tea and eating biscuits.

"There, now," she said with satisfaction, dipping a generous serving of steaming stew into a bowl. "You eat that, you old mule."

"It's too much," Peter protested.

"I'll say when it's too much," Sarah said threateningly. "Come on, Judith. We'd best leave, or we'll never make it home before dark." She turned back to Uncle Peter. "I'm sending Frank or Henry up here tomorrow if it don't snow. You'd best have finished that jar of stew."

"Good-bye, Uncle Peter," Judith said, bending down to brush his wrinkled cheek with her lips.

"Who is it?" he asked, peering at her owlishly.

"I'm Judith."

"Wesley's oldest gal," Aunt Sarah said, shoving her toward the door.

"Do you think he'll be all right?" Judith asked anxiously, when they were in the wagon.

"He doesn't look healthy," Sarah admitted, lifting the reins. "I meant it when I said Frank or Henry needs to come up here. He may not want to be with people, but I think the time has come."

*****

When Judith and the children got home at last, Christina was in the kitchen, mixing biscuit dough. She and Ned had milked the cows and fed the stock, and Ned had brought Chub's harness into the kitchen, where he sat on the floor cleaning it. Judith was glad he had found something useful to do. She put her apron on and set to work helping Christina get supper ready.

"Sorry we're so late. I went with Aunt Sarah to Uncle Peter's. That was quite an adventure."

"I can barely remember what he looks like," Christina mused. "Did he talk to you?"

"Oh, yes. I think his stomach may be bothering him. He hasn't been eating well."

"Did he like the quilt?"

"Hard to say, but I think so. Oh, that reminds me, I got some information for you."

Christina took the cover off the baking powder can and began cutting round biscuits with it. "What is it?"

"Nancy Farwell had her baby."

"I heard that already. It's a boy. Elmer Ormond Farwell." Christina grimaced as she recited the name.

"Oh," said Judith. "Well, Mrs. Sibley is going to be a hundred years old next week. Did you know that?"

"No. That's amazing."

"Isn't it? I think you should write a story about her. Ask Mr. Thayer. You could interview her and find out what she remembers from when she was little. It would be fascinating. Ask her how she keeps so spry, and what her best and worst memories are, that sort of thing."

"That's a great idea for next week. I'll talk to B—Mr. Thayer. Today was my deadline, and Ned and I took my news up to him this afternoon. I finished writing up my interview with Professor Montgomery. I guarantee that story will interest you."

"I can hardly wait to see it in print," said Judith.

# Chapter 11

Judith greeted Bud Hofses at the door eagerly on Saturday.

"What have you got for me?"

"Oh, nothing much." His eyes twinkled. "Just a postcard from your daddy...and a telegram from the Army camp."

"Thank you so much!" Judith tore the envelope open and smiled at him. "Joel is coming home Monday, Mr. Hofses."

"You're giving me the scoop, not saving it for the *Hummer*?" Bud asked.

Judith laughed. "You'll always be the fastest way to spread news around this town!"

Bud sobered. "Too bad about Harry Gardner. His daddy's gone to Lewiston to bring him home on the train."

"It's so sad," Judith murmured.

"Yes. Funeral's tomorrow."

She pulled her coat on when he had left and took Lydia with her for a brisk walk up the road to Ben's house. The snow had held off, but the sky was a brooding gray, and a keen wind blew off the river.

"It's official," she told Ben when he came to the door. "Joel's coming in Monday. I don't know if it's too late to get it in the *Hummer* or not, but I wanted to tell you, anyway."

"I've laid out the front page," he told her, "but I'll add it to Christina's neighborhood news inside. Private Joel Chadbourne is expected home on Monday. What train?"

"The 2:15."

"Great. I'll deliver the papers in the morning and pick you up at 1:30."

"Thank you. You really don't have to—"

"I want Joel to get home quickly, and if it's cold, a five-mile ride in an open wagon could really set him back."

She nodded. "I really appreciate it."

"Come in for a cup of coffee, Judith. You've got Lydia here..."

"No, thanks just the same."

He nodded, as though it was what he had expected.

"Bud Hofses just told me Harry's funeral is tomorrow," she said.

"Yes. Two o'clock at church."

"Joel will be sorry he missed it."

"Well, maybe it's better this way. If he were home, he'd insist on going out to the cemetery in the cold." Ben shrugged. "Can I give you and the children a ride?"

"No, thank you. We'll be fine."

When she got home, Uncle Frank's wagon was in the yard, and her uncle was in the kitchen with Ned and Bobby. The boys had poured milk for three and served soft molasses cookies.

Uncle Frank smiled sheepishly, his mouth full.

"Well, well, three scamps raiding my cookie jar." Judith laughed.

Frank swallowed. "Good cookies."

"Grandma's recipe," she said, reaching for one.

"Judith, we wanted you to know Uncle Peter is with us now."

"What happened?" she asked.

"Sarah told me he was looking peaked, so Henry and I went up this morning, and he was huddled in his bed with the fire most out. Seemed to have a fever. We bundled him up and took him to the house, and I had Doc Stearns in to see him."

"Is he going to be all right?"

"He's a tough old bird. I was afraid it was pneumonia, but the doc says not. Anyway, he'll stay with us at least through the winter, then he can go back to the woods if he wants to. But we didn't want him to die alone back there."

Judith nodded. "I'm glad. I think he needs a little care."

"Sarah will coddle him," Frank said. "She acts bossy, but she has a tender heart. You and the kids come over and see him. Not all at once, that would shake him up, but I think in small doses he'd like to see you. He asked about you this morning."

"Did he really?" Judith smiled in surprise.

"Yes, wanted to know where that pretty gal of Wesley's was. I told him to behave and you'd come round to see him. Of course, Sarah chimed in and said he had to have a bath and a haircut first."

Judith chuckled. "Aunt Sarah will have him towing the line in a hurry."

"Well, she's efficient," Frank conceded. "I don't say Peter doesn't need it."

A few flakes were fluttering down when he left, and by morning six inches of wet, sticky snow lay on the ground, and more was falling. Judith was trying to decide whether or not to strike out for church or stay home that morning when Ben drove in with Chester and his sleigh.

"If you're going to church, I insist on taking you," he said. Judith hesitated, and he added, "No one is going to gossip, Judith. There's the funeral this afternoon, and I thought I'd take my car then if the roads aren't too bad, but it doesn't make sense for such close neighbors to take two rigs out in this weather for church."

She gave in, and was especially grateful when he came in the Oldsmobile that afternoon to take them back to the church for the funeral. By then, the roads were packed down enough for the car to get through without problems.

Christina wept profusely during the service, hiding her face behind her handkerchief and her gloved hands. Lydia and Bobby cried, too, and Ned sat, stoic but moist-eyed, staring straight ahead.

The casket would go to the crypt at the cemetery, to await spring burial. Ben offered to drive them to the Gardners' home, where relatives and neighbors would gather with Harry's family. She didn't think Christina could stand the strain of trying to contain her grief before such a crowd.

"I think we should go right home," Judith told him. "The children ..."

He nodded. "I'll drop you off and make a brief stop at the Gardners'."

She nodded gratefully.

*****

By noon the next day, traffic and warmth had nearly cleared the road. Ben arrived at the Chadbourne house at 1:30.

"I hope you didn't send Christina and the children in the sled this morning," he said to Judith.

"No, they wanted to take it, but it looked to me like the snow was melting, so I made them take the wagon. I hope it doesn't end up too slushy, or it will be hard going for Lady this afternoon."

Ben was quiet on the way to the train depot, and Judith's mood seemed to match his. The funeral had depressed them all. She couldn't shake off a fear that something would go wrong, and Joel would not be on the train.

They were a few minutes early and sat in the car facing the platform, waiting.

"How's your father?" Ben asked, watching out the side window.

"Better, I'm glad to say. He's sending most of his pay every week, and he'll come home for a few days at Christmas. They intend to finish the ship they're working on, but he's not sure if the job will last when that one's done."

"Do you think it's time to put the guns back in the closet?"

"Probably."

Ben nodded. "I'll take care of it when we get home. And how have *you* been?"

"Fine." She tried to think of something else to say, but her old shyness with him returned. At last she said, "Christina's story on the professor surprised me."

"Interesting, wasn't it?"

"Fascinating," she said. "All that about how mathematics helped win the war."

Ben smiled. "Well, a lot of things helped win the war. But I agree, he made it simple to understand how important it is to have good engineers and mathematicians. And Christina wrote it up well, so it was an appealing story. I hope it inspired some youngsters."

"I'm proud of her."

He nodded, and they sat in silence again. After several minutes, Judith asked, "Did you deliver the papers today?"

"I took most of them around this morning."

"You must have been up at dawn to finish the printing and deliver them."

"I've got a few to take round later." He shifted to look at her profile. "Thank you for letting me help you."

Judith inhaled carefully. "I think I'm learning about helping others and … and love."

His eyebrows shot up. "How's that?"

"Well, when you love someone, you help them whether they want it or not." She knew her cheeks were flaming. "I mean—well, there's my Uncle Peter, for instance. My great uncle, really." She looked up at Ben, hoping desperately that he wouldn't misunderstand her. That would be mortifying. "He's lived all alone for twenty years, and he didn't want anyone to fuss over him, but he's very old now, and he can't be alone. So Uncle Frank just picked him up and took him home with him."

Ben nodded soberly. "It's difficult to do something like that, when the person wants to be independent."

"Yes. And Joel may be that way. I don't want him to feel helpless, but he'll have to depend on us all for a while. And some other time, when he's healthy again, it might be me who has to depend on him." She shrugged at her inability to express her feeling. "Do you understand?"

"Oh, yes, I do."

Judith nodded. He was so grave, she believed he really did understand her turmoil. "You don't know Joel very well, but you've been a wonderful friend to him. To me." She nodded judiciously. "To all of us. And I thank you."

Ben was silent a moment. In the distance, the train whistle sounded. "You're welcome," he said softly, and he turned to look down the tracks.

*****

The reunion with Joel was jubilant. The children had rushed home from school and were waiting impatiently when Ben's car arrived. Ben let Joel lean on his shoulder as far as the sofa in the front room and carried his bag in, then quietly took his leave.

Joel was weak and pale, and sat on the sofa gathering his strength.

Ned and Lydia peppered him with questions, and Bobby snuggled beside him, asking repeatedly, "You all right, Joel?"

Judith brought him a glass of cider and a plate of cookies.

"Think you can get me up the stairs?" he asked anxiously.

"I'm putting you in the den for a while, until you feel up to doing the stairs, all right?"

Joel frowned. "I suppose, if you think that's best." The den was a small room downstairs, where their mother had slept when babies were born, and where any sick family members were placed for the duration of the illness.

"Well, if you want to be in your room, we'll see what we can do, but—"

"I'm pretty wobbly," he admitted. "Maybe I'll stay down here tonight, and we can see how I feel tomorrow."

Judith was afraid the little boys would wear him out with their questions and excitement. Christina had the second edition of the *Hummer* ready to show him, with her byline on the turkey story and the profile of the mathematics professor. They wanted to show him everything, but Judith finally got them to leave him alone in the den so he could have a nap before supper.

He stayed close to home all week, going out to the barn with the boys at chore time. Only two cows were giving any milk now, and the milking was finished quickly. Even Ned could do it. Joel sat close to the stove most of the day while the children were at school, and by Friday felt strong enough to walk up to Ben's house for a short visit. Judith watched the road anxiously through the dining room window for his return, and in an hour he was back, tired, but encouraged from his talk with Ben and the knowledge that he was healing.

New snow fell that night, and the next morning Aunt Alla drove into the yard in a pung, with her spotted mare in harness.

"Now, I'm just making a dooryard call," she insisted, when Judith stepped out to greet her. "I wanted to see Joel and bring you a little something."

Joel came to the barn door and waved. He walked slowly across the yard toward her, and the younger boys raced past him, whooping at their aunt.

"Now, settle down, Ned, Bobby," Judith scolded. "You'll spook Adelaide. You know better than that."

"They're getting so big," Alla declared. "Here, Bobby, you take this oatmeal bread inside, and Ned, you get the beanpot. There, Judith, you don't have to cook tonight."

"Thank you, Auntie. That's very kind."

Joel had reached the sled by then, and stooped to kiss Alla.

"Bless you, dear boy," she said. "Thank God you're home. We prayed a sight for you."

"Thanks, Auntie. I appreciate that."

"You're too thin," she said critically. "Judith, you feed this boy."

"I will."

"See that you do. I should have brought a pie."

"I'll make pies this morning," Judith promised.

"Where's your hat, Joel?" Alla asked sharply.

"In the barn. I was cleaning out, and I got too warm."

Alla shook her head. "Well, it's not too warm out here. Best put it on." Adelaide was stirring restlessly. "All right, old thing, let's go." She lifted the reins, and Adelaide leaned into her collar and headed eagerly for the road.

*****

Judith thought Joel was too frail to make the trip to church on Sunday, but Ben offered to take him to the worship service in his car. Judith took the children in the wagon, leaving at nine o'clock for Sunday school. It was cold, and she heated two soapstones on the wood stove and wrapped them in newspaper and towels to help the children keep warm on the way. Ben and Joel came in after Sunday school, and Ben sat beside Joel on the end of the Chadbournes' pew.

When they came out of the church at noon, it was snowing again. Chub trotted all the way home, snorting and shaking his head. Ben drove Joel home, and took Christina and Bobby in the car as well. His automobile was still at the house when Judith, Ned and Lydia got home with the wagon.

"I invited him to stay for dinner," Christina confided when Judith scurried into the kitchen.

Judith was startled. "But we're not prepared for company."

"Of course we are," her sister chided. "We've been baking all sorts of goodies for Joel. We have plenty, and the house is spotless. Judith, it's the least we can do."

Shame washed over her. She was letting her timidity prompt her to rudeness. "You're right. He's done so much for us. I should have thought of it myself."

She found it hard to eat with Ben across the table. He, Joel, and Christina kept a lively conversation flowing, but Judith was quiet. She missed her parents terribly. They should have been there for a happy meal with all the children. Ben didn't seem to feel the awkwardness that she did, but somehow Judith couldn't quite allow herself to be happy, even with Joel home.

Ben's presence only made things worse. Did he think she was doing an adequate job with her housekeeping and child rearing? He approved of her cooking; that much was obvious when he took seconds and complimented her gravy. He divided his attention among the children, and she was grateful for that. But the gentle smile he occasionally turned her way was anything but soothing to Judith. Her anxiety rose every time he looked down the table at her.

# Chapter 12

Joel began driving the children to school in the wagon or the sled, and picking them up after. Judith worried about him at first, but he seemed to gain strength from being out in the cold air. After school, he drove Christina around to talk to people. She was building up a list of contacts who could be counted on to steer her toward interesting happenings.

The second week, Joel went to see Harry Gardner's parents. Judith almost protested, but made herself keep quiet. He needs to do this, she told herself. Joel came back subdued and retired to his room until chore time.

Ethelwynn, the patient cow, calved early, on December tenth, replenishing their milk supply just as Edith and Gwendoline were drying up. The little calf was weak, but the boys took him into the house. He lay in the kitchen on feed sacks that night, near the cook stove. By morning he was on his feet and hungry.

Joel christened him Jack Dempsey. "He's a real fighter," he explained. He carried Jack to the barn, and reintroduced him to his mother. A week later, Joel had taken over the milking and saw that the boys did the rest of the chores. Judith rarely had to go to the barn anymore. And Joel spent many hours at the Thayer house.

"What do you do up there?" Judith asked him. She couldn't imagine Ben stopping his work for long. He wasn't one to waste time talking.

"Sometimes I clean the type for him," Joel said. "Today he showed me how to set up for printing telephone bills."

Judith laughed. "We don't have telephones out here, but we can serve the telephone company."

"Ben's getting one soon, and if they bring the lines to his house, we'll have one, too."

"I've heard that before."

Joel shrugged. "I believe it. Ben knows one of the head men at the telephone company. When the weather breaks in the spring, we'll have it."

"If we can afford it."

"Well, Ben says when the *Hummer's* circulation is a little higher, he'll give me a job. Then things will be easier. You'll see."

Judith shook her head. "Sometimes I think he started the *Hummer* just for us."

"He's having fun with it."

"Exactly. It's just a hobby for him."

"Everybody should be able to earn a living doing something they enjoy."

"He's not earning a living at that," Judith scoffed. She was amazed at the surge of conflicting emotions the little newspaper aroused in her heart. *I'll take that as a challenge,* Ben had said, as though it rankled him that she thought it would fail. She hadn't meant to upset him, but she'd been uncomfortable with the notion that a man was launching a precarious business just to help her family. If he lost money on the venture, would he go on printing it, just so he'd have an excuse to pay Christina? Was it charity, or wasn't it? He'd paid her sister three dollars and eighty cents last week, and Christina had been euphoric over her wages. Judith couldn't help feeling the *Hummer* was his way to slip some desperately-needed cash to the Chadbournes. Never mind that without it she wouldn't have been able to replace Ned's ragged shoes.

"He earns his living with his magazine drawings," she insisted. "The *Hummer* is not a profit maker, believe me."

"Ben says it will be soon."

"Pardon me for being skeptical."

"Why is it you don't like him?" Joel asked.

"I—I do like him." Judith felt her face redden. She hadn't meant to belittle Ben and his enterprise.

"Funny," said Joel. "I never would have known. You contradict everything he says."

Judith turned away in confusion. "He's different from us. But I like him."

Twice on printing days, Joel took Ned and Bobby to Ben's to sort type after school, and it seemed to Judith that Ben was fast becoming a hero to all the boys. Lydia complained that she never got to be in on the fun.

"It's work," Ned said proudly.

"I need you right here," Judith told Lydia, but she couldn't help feeling a little envious herself. The boys got to see the wonders of the Thayer house. They probably took for granted beautiful sights she had never seen. And they spent time with Ben himself.

She tried not to think that his company would be a drawing card for her, too. Despite Joel's assessment of her attitude toward Ben, she knew she admired him tremendously. She was still a bit in awe of him, and her nerves inevitably kicked up when he spoke to her. She was sure he considered her a bit too prim for a twentieth-century woman, and that irked her. A meeting with Ben Thayer was anything but restful.

\*\*\*\*\*

Snow fell heavily in mid-December, and school let out early for Christmas vacation. The roads were blocked for days, until oxen waded through, pulling a roller to pack the snow behind them. The Chadbournes began riding to church in the sleigh.

The Friday before Christmas, Judith worked hard all day at cleaning and baking. They expected Pa to come home the next day. Joel took Christina in the sleigh to ferret out the neighborhood news, and Judith set the younger children tasks in the house. In the late afternoon, she let the boys go out to tunnel in the snow and allowed Lydia to make paper chains for the Christmas tree she hoped they would soon have in the front room.

She heard the sleigh return, and Ned and Bobby ran to the barn to help Joel with the evening chores. The sun was long down and supper was ready when the three boys came in from the barn.

Judith looked up as Ned closed the back door. "Joel, where is Christina?"

"I dropped her off at Ben's. She should be here soon."

"You dropped her off two hours ago? Joel, something's not right."

He shrugged. "You want me to run up there?"

"No," Judith said stonily, "I'm going myself." She pulled on her coat, hat and gloves.

"Why are you so mad?" Joel asked. "Ben employs her. You know he's trustworthy."

"It's the principle," Judith said archly. "Mr. Thayer and I discussed the situation weeks ago, and he promised not to let Christina become the object of gossip."

"Judith, he's a friend of the family." Joel's voice was tight with exasperation.

She wavered for an instant. Ben had shown himself to be a caring neighbor, it was true. But still, there were rules of conduct that a gentleman would never break, out of respect for a lady. She wouldn't allow the erratic feelings for Ben that had recently troubled her enter into it. This was something she must do for her parents' sake.

"If Mother were here," she began, but Joel's impatient gesture stopped her cold. He was nineteen, and Ben had become his friend and idol, she could see that. She wasn't sure it was a good thing, if Ben was going to blur the lines between gentility and ill behavior.

"You and the children go ahead and eat," she said coldly.

As she walked determinedly the four hundred yards up the snowy road from her driveway to Ben's, her anger cooled somewhat in the frigid air, to a throbbing hurt. Ben had presumed on their fragile friendship. She had made her convictions clear, but they weren't important to him. She tried to plan what she would say, knowing her words and her tone might dictate the future of their relationship.

She strode up his front steps onto the piazza and knocked loudly on the front door. A few seconds later he opened it.

"Judith! Come right in. What can I do for you?"

"Is Christina here?"

"Yes, she's in the print shop. Is everything all right?" Concern came over his face.

Judith sighed impatiently. "No, everything is not all right, Mr. Thayer. My brother left Christina here two hours ago. She was supposed to give you her stories and come right home. You know I don't want her here alone. I expressly asked you not to do this."

His expression had changed to guilt and regret. "I'm sorry, Judith. She had the interview with Mrs. Sibley, and it needed some rewriting, and I just wanted to help her a little, show her how to do it professionally. Then she started cleaning type for me, and I just—well, I forgot. I'm truly sorry. I assure you—"

"Hi, Judith!" Christina appeared in the doorway to the parlor. "Ben helped me with my interview, and it really reads well now!"

Christina's blithe disregard for propriety brought Judith's indignation back to the surface. Somehow, she had failed with Christina. She had fed the family and kept them in decent clothes, seen their father through his time of depression, had given them all a clean home and, yes, a loving heart, but she had neglected to instill the importance of virtue in her younger sister.

"I'm sure it does. Please get your things and come home."

"Judith—" Ben began.

She shook her head. "I am not happy, Mr. Thayer. If you want to discuss this, perhaps we should wait until tomorrow. I might say something I would regret if we go into it now."

He looked down at the floor. Judith felt a smidgen of shame, but her resentment overpowered it. When Christina came with her coat, hat and schoolbooks, Judith drew her onto the piazza and turned to face Ben.

"I thought we had some rules for the reporting staff of the *Hummer*. If you can't live with my terms, Mr. Thayer, I'm sorry, but I'll have to—"

He held up his hands in protest. "As you said, Judith, let's let this rest overnight. I'll come see you tomorrow. We'll discuss it calmly."

She nodded curtly and marched out with Christina in tow. They walked silently in the crisp night with only starlight on the snow to guide them.

As they reached the Chadbourne driveway, Christina said tearfully, "You were terribly rude, Judith."

"Ha!"

"He is my boss, and he is my friend, and he is decent and trustworthy."

Christina ran crying up the stairs to her bedroom. Judith felt like crying herself, but she made herself breathe deeply and go to the kitchen to join the others for supper.

When she fell into bed that night, she lay for a long time staring at the gray rectangle formed by the window. She said her usual prayers, but the situation still felt wrong. Was all of this pride? She wanted to protect her sister and the family. Did she have to make Christina stop reporting to do that?

Tears began to flow, and she turned her face into her pillow so no one would hear her crying. Was it Ben who had infuriated her, or was it herself? The newspaper had given Christina something to motivate her, and Judith had even thought it kept her from falling into despair after Harry's death. And now she was threatening to take that away from her.

*Dear Lord,* she sobbed, *if I have to be mother and sister to these children, I need more wisdom and patience.*

Over the weeks, her confusion had mounted, and now it had reached a zenith. Ben was throwing her world into chaos, but was it his fault, or was it her own youth and foolishness? Were his overtures merely the duty of a neighbor, or were they something more? She had come to hope they represented friendship. Now she faced the fact that her own feelings had bounded past friendliness.

It frightened her to admit her affections were deeply fastened on him. Had she any cause to feel this way? And had she any right to be disappointed in him now?

He was so much older than her, and surely he was wiser, too. The more she thought about it, the more she felt he must view her much the way she saw Christina—young, inexperienced, unpolished, and perhaps at times unreasonable.

Was this sticking point of manners and propriety worth losing his friendship over? She feared she had made it into a banner of adulthood and waved it in Ben's face, demanding that he see her as an equal. She desperately wanted his respect. She was, after all, a woman, not a child. On their trip to Lewiston, she had felt that he treated her as a woman. It had been exhilarating, but a little frightening. Now ... how was he thinking of her now that she had scolded him petulantly for his inadvertent lapse of courtesy?

She rolled onto her back and sniffed, staring at the window again. If Mother were here, she decided, this wouldn't be such a huge crisis. Mother would handle it deftly but unobtrusively. She would chide Christina, perhaps, and Ben would receive a gentle reminder that appearances mattered. But Mother would never, never rant at a neighbor.

She closed her aching eyes and added one last petition to her prayer. *And let me be at peace ... with Ben, Lord.*

# Chapter 13

Ben fed his horse and groomed him patiently the next morning, thinking of how he would deal with Judith's ire. As he combed the tangles from Chester's mane, he saw her clearly, her gray eyes at the same time accusing and wounded. She was beautiful in her fury. Her deep golden hair had glimmered in the lamplight, and her sharp words had cut him deeply.

He hadn't expected to be ambushed by love again. She was so young. Too young? He didn't think so, but he still wrestled with that. It startled him to find how deeply she had worked her way into his heart, when he had thought it was sealed forever.

The Chadbournes' grief and impending poverty had drawn him to her at first, but her staunch determination to hold the family together had raised his admiration considerably. Judith had grit, and she was resolved not to let her mother down.

That was it, he realized in a flash. She was trying to set for her younger sisters the example she thought her mother would set. Mrs. Chadbourne wouldn't have stormed his castle gate and dragged Christina off in a rage, but Judith thought correctly that her mother wouldn't want her sixteen-year-old daughter alone with a man—any man—for two hours. It was thoughtless of him, in the extreme. The last thing he wanted now was to cause Judith distress.

He walked down the road to River Rest. The farmhouse needed paint. If Wesley didn't initiate the job this spring, maybe he could plant the seed in Joel's mind.

Judith received him in her parlor, standing rigid, her hands clasped nervously, her eyes not quite meeting his.

"Mr. Thayer—"

Before she could light into him again, Ben stepped forward, holding his hat. "Judith, forgive me. You were right. Every word you said last night was true."

Her lower lip trembled. "It was?"

"Yes. You told me your concerns before, and I took them seriously. Last night I just overlooked them, and that was unconscionable. Please don't make Christina stop working for me. She's helping the family with the money she earns, isn't she?"

"Yes, you know she is." Judith hung her head. "I let her keep half of it. I'm hoping she can save some and maybe go to college. But she can't work if her reputation is going to suffer."

"I understand that. Truly. Again, I beg you to forgive me. I just wasn't thinking." A tear clung to her eyelashes, and Ben was emboldened to thrash the issue out with her. "Judith, there's nothing … unhealthy … in my relationship to Christina, I assure you. Of course, outsiders wouldn't know that. But she's very bright, and I enjoy working with her. I tell her something once, and I know she'll remember and carry that through in the next piece she writes. Unfortunately, I'm a little slower, I guess."

She crumpled a handful of the material of her heavy blue skirt. "Mr. Thayer, I don't mistrust you. I just have to think of what's best for Christina. Earning money is good, but having respect in this community is crucial."

"I understand."

Judith raised her eyes to his. "Do you?"

"Yes. My own mother wouldn't want my sisters to behave so."

She swallowed. "Thank you."

"Perhaps I have a solution to this predicament," Ben offered, watching her anxiously. If she showed the least bit of animosity he would retreat, but she stood waiting, her cheeks slightly reddened, and her eyes moist, her lips pressed tightly together, so he went on. "Now that the war is over, I can get paper easier, and prices are coming down. I'm thinking of expanding the *Hummer* to eight pages next week. But I still have other printing jobs to do, and drawings on commission. I thought perhaps I'd hire Joel to help me in the print shop if he wants to. He's done some small jobs, just as a favor, and he shows aptitude for it. I might eventually put him in charge of advertising."

Judith shook her head. "Joel has work here on the farm."

"But it's slow right now, in the winter. You can spare him a couple of days a week."

He thought he saw suspicion and anxiety in her eyes as she lifted her chin. "Joel doesn't want to be a printer. He'll own this farm someday. He wants to farm."

"Are you sure?" She winced, and he wondered if he had hit a tender spot. "You speak of sending Christina to college. What about Joel?"

"I—Father never—" She stopped and looked away for a second, then back again. "I don't know," she admitted. "Joel has never talked to me about doing anything else. I guess I've assumed he liked farming."

"I think he does," Ben said gently, "but it wouldn't hurt him to learn a trade as well. He has a mechanical bent, and seems to enjoy working in my shop. The press jammed the other day. He had it apart and fixed before I even knew what had happened. I'll employ him until spring planting, Judith. When he's needed for the farm work, I won't hold him."

"He'll need to cut wood for next winter."

"Fine, then, two days a week, or whatever he can spare me."

"How can you do this?"

"Do what?" She was so earnest, his heart lurched a bit. He longed to protect her from hardship and anything that wasn't fine and beautiful.

"You pull jobs out of thin air so we won't lose the farm," Judith choked.

"Is that what you think I'm doing?"

She blushed. "It's crossed my mind. I don't know *why* you would do it."

He couldn't help smiling. "Well, it may disappoint you, but the *Hummer* broke even this week."

"It did?"

"Yes. We have thirty subscriptions now, and we sold another fifty copies through stores. And I took in seventeen dollars for ads. That means the Hummer is more than paying for its ink, paper, and reporter's wages. Barely, I admit, but it's growing. I need an assistant in the shop badly on printing days."

"Incredible," she said. "So soon."

"You really didn't think I could do it, did you?"

"I thought you'd go bankrupt over it."

He laughed. "Are you disappointed? Oh, Judith, you are far too pessimistic. You need a little frivolity in your life."

She stared at him, and he thought for a moment she would cry. He hadn't meant to make fun of her.

She looked away first, frowning. "Joel will need to start cutting firewood as soon as he's strong enough."

"Let me talk to him," Ben said hastily. "If he'll come on Fridays, Saturdays, and Mondays, I'll have the help I need on my busiest days, and it will be safe for Christina to bring her copy in on those days. If she needs to see me at other times, she can bring Ned or Lydia. I'll lay down the law to her. We'll abide by it. And if Joel needs help with the wood, I'll help him on Tuesdays."

"Oh, no! You couldn't do that!" Her gray eyes were more troubled than ever.

"Why not? You think I'm helpless? I can swing an ax."

"That's not what I meant. You're so busy."

"Maybe I've been *too* busy. I want to do this. Besides, I can use the exercise." A minor guilt was nagging him again. He'd bought his winter's wood all sawn and split, glad to have more time to spend inside at the press and his drawing board this year. But he missed the manual labor, if the truth were told. It would do him good to get out in the woods again with Joel and do some physical work. It would also keep fresh in his mind how hard his neighbors worked for their most basic needs.

Judith opened her mouth, then took a deep breath and turned suddenly away from him, toward the window.

"Is that all right?" he asked softly.

He thought her shoulders quivered. Beyond the window, a blue jay was dominating the bird feeder, keeping the chickadees and grosbeaks at bay while it pecked at the suet and corn.

"Yes," she said at last, barely more than a sigh.

"Good." They stood there awkwardly for a moment. She didn't turn around, and he wondered if the capitulation had brought her to tears. He stepped nearer and touched her sleeve lightly, tentatively. She caught her breath and took a step toward the window.

"Thank you, Judith." Best to leave her alone now. He turned and walked toward the front door.

"Joel is in the barn," she called after him.

He swung around and looked her in the face. Something seemed to flare up in her eyes as she met his direct gaze for an instant, before she looked down in confusion. "You can go out through the kitchen."

He nodded and went past her to the kitchen and out the back door. Striding quickly along the ell, he was soon on the threshing floor of the big barn. Joel had Chub out of his stall, hitched to the wall with a lead rope, and was brushing him.

"Your father's got a nice setup here," Ben called in greeting.

"Ben! What brings you here?"

"Your sister, what else?"

Joel laughed. "She was steamed last night! Don't let her boss you around."

"She's just doing her job," Ben said evenly.

Joel worked his way around the horse to brush his off side. Ben laid a hand on Chub's withers. "You're going to meet your father today?"

"No, just killing time. He said he had a ride. I'm not sure when he'll show up, so I'm just trying to stay out of Judith's way this morning. Sometimes she can be a regular harpy, and she was pretty snappish over breakfast."

Ben smiled. "My fault, I guess. But I think she and I have reached an understanding."

Joel looked at him quickly. "What kind of understanding?"

"Not that kind," Ben said ruefully. "She still thinks I'm a bit sinister, I'm afraid. But she's agreed to let me to take you on part time, if you're willing, for the print shop. Christina can bring her articles to me while you're at the house."

Joel nodded. "I'd like that, and the regular hours would mollify Judith. I should have realized last night how upset she'd be, but I didn't. Hate to think she was right, but I ought to have brought Christina home when I came."

"Yes. Well, it won't happen again."

"I gathered that." Joel shook his head. "None of my business, but you're putting up with a lot from my sister."

"I'd put up with a lot more."

"Too bad, in a way," Joel said regretfully.

"She's a beauty."

The boy stared at him and said cautiously, "There's worse, I suppose, but doesn't temperament count for something?"

"Joel, if you weren't her brother, you'd see things differently." Ben strolled to the big barn door and rolled it open an couple of inches. Judith was outside at the bird feeder, adding corn to the tray. The blue jay kept its distance while she worked, but the little chickadees landed on the feeder and the branch above, and one even alit momentarily on her hood.

She went back into the house, and Ben closed the door. He picked up a rag and began to polish Chub's near flank. "Ninety-nine percent of the time, she's meek as a lamb. Fear can masquerade as anger, you know."

"Fear? Judith's not afraid of anything."

"Oh, yes, she is, my friend. She's afraid of making mistakes, and not living up to her mother's memory, and somehow letting the family fall apart. She's afraid of life, pure and simple. She needs to sort that out, and I'm trying to be patient."

Joel stood up and looked hard at him across the gelding's back for a moment. "Got it bad, haven't you?"

# Chapter 14

Merton Hammond's sleigh turned in to the dooryard just before noon, and Pa climbed out and reached for his bag. Before he had his luggage out, all six children surrounded him.

He hugged the young ones and brushed them off, letting Ned take his bag, then turned to face his oldest son.

"Well, Joel. You don't look so bad."

Joel stepped up and shook his father's hand awkwardly. "Thanks, Father. I'm glad you're home."

Judith stepped up then and put her arms around her father's neck, kissing him below his eye, on the smooth spot where the whiskers didn't grow. "Come on in, Father. You're tired. I've got a nice lunch ready, then you can relax."

Merton Hammond raised his whip in salute and urged the horse up. The Chadbournes waved, calling their thanks to him.

Pa was thin and subdued, but more alert than he had been in the fall. He seemed to have kept his purpose during his absence, and he brought eighty dollars home with him.

"Keep out what you need, Judith, and put the rest in the bank," he told her. She kept out twenty dollars and set the rest aside.

He had brought Christmas gifts for the young ones, and he gave them into her safekeeping. Judith hid them in her room. Slingshots for Ned and Bobby, and a doll for Lydia. He asked Judith to purchase clothing for herself and Christina, and a suit for Joel.

"We don't need much, Father," she said. "We need to save as much as we can for the taxes."

"Get what you girls need," he insisted. "Joel will be twenty soon. He needs a suit."

So she did as he asked, and the gifts were ready and wrapped.

Her father spent hours in the barn with Joel. She knew they had discussed trading a heifer to a neighbor for a small flock of sheep. Joel wanted to try raising a few sheep, and Christina was his ally in persuading their father.

"As long as you don't expect me to spin the wool," Judith had told them. Now Joel was fixing a pen in the barn for the sheep, and a lambing stall.

Once when she went to the clothesline, Judith saw Ben come out of the barn. She knew her father and brother were there, and wondered if he had come on business or pleasure. He didn't come to the house, so she didn't ask.

Joel put the two small boys on a sled and pulled them down to the lower pasture, where a stand of balsam firs grew. Lydia and Christina insisted on donning high boots and following. The snow's crust was hard enough for them to walk on in most places, though they occasionally broke through and floundered to their knees.

They came back rosy-cheeked and laughing, and Joel dragged their Christmas tree by the stump into the barn. His father joined him to help fit it with a stand, and then they carried it into the parlor. They braced it, and it stood in a corner, resplendent with their homemade decorations.

"Where's the star?" Lydia cried when the last ornament was in place.

Judith caught her breath. "I—I broke it."

"You broke it?" Lydia snapped.

"Yes. I'm sorry." She looked at her father ruefully. "It was my own fault. I was in a hurry to get something, and I knocked it on the floor."

"Clumsy!" Ned cried accusingly.

"Leave it alone, Ned," said Joel. "She couldn't help it."

Judith threw him a grateful glance.

"What's done is done," their father said. "Let's not fuss about it, Ned."

Little Bobby smiled tremulously up at his oldest sister. "We forgive you, Judith."

She knelt and embraced him. "Thank you, Bobby. I've been feeling bad about it, but I didn't have a chance to tell Father."

"Maybe we can put something else up there," said Christina, but no one could think what, so the tip of the fir tree remained bare.

Joel came in late to supper on Christmas Eve, and paused in the front room before joining the family at the dining table. When the meal was over, the children pestered Judith and Christina to hurry with the dishes so they could have their gifts. As she put the last of the silverware away, Judith shooed them out of the kitchen.

"I'll be right there," she promised. She hung up her apron and looked around the room. The kitchen was as neat as her mother would have left it.

When she entered the parlor, she smiled at the children. Only her mother's loving face was missing. That, and—she gasped as she looked at tree. At the top was a flat star as big as her spread hand, black, with a scene outlined in a few lines of gleaming gold paint. Heavenly light fell on the village of Bethlehem. It was simple, but its beauty took her breath away.

"Where did that come from?" she asked, but she knew.

"Ben made it," said Joel. "He almost didn't send it down. He was afraid you wouldn't like it. But we needed something."

Judith stood very still, gazing at the scene that spoke so eloquently to her of peace on earth, and in the family, although it would never be the same without her mother. A hopeful longing flickered in her heart.

Ned brought the family Bible to his father, and Wesley read the story of the nativity from Luke chapter two and asked a blessing on the family. Joel distributed the family's gifts, then handed each a small package wrapped in white tissue paper.

"From Ben," he said quietly, placing a larger, flat parcel in Judith's hands.

Her face went scarlet. The white tissue paper had intricate snowflakes all over it, and she realized suddenly he had drawn them individually in ink. It must have taken him hours to embellish the wrapping paper. She removed it carefully and smoothed it out, setting it aside. A picture frame was face down in her lap. She turned it over slowly. It was about ten inches by fourteen, and the gold sides surrounded a painting of maple leaves, close up, blazing at her in orange and yellow, crimson and apricot.

"Oh, gorgeous," Christina exclaimed. She took it from Judith's nerveless fingers and passed it around the circle.

Judith sat without moving. A dull ache in her chest made it hard to breathe. How could he know so surely what would bring her joy? It was alarming. A snatch of conversation came back to her. *Winter's coming. I miss the leaves.* Ben had remembered that, had turned it into a gift for her. She wrapped that knowledge around her as she had her cape on that chilly day.

When the painting came back to her, she took it and the tissue paper up to her room. Slowly, she took down the print that had hung on her bedroom wall since she was a child—Little Bo Peep. She hung the flaming maple leaves in its place, and stood back to appraise them. Amazing how real they looked, when in the fall she had thought how artificial the brightly colored leaves seemed.

Opening her top dresser drawer, she pulled out her clean clothes and the newspaper she had lined the drawer with last spring. She laid the tissue paper carefully in the bottom of the drawer, then replaced her clothing.

She slipped back downstairs. Christina jumped up and showed her the mechanical pencil Ben had sent for her. Bobby, Ned, and Lydia had candy, and Joel and his father had leather pocket diaries. Mr. Chadbourne looked at all their gifts in confusion.

"Mr. Thayer sent all of these things?" he asked.

"Yes, father. He's become a good friend," Judith said. "Christina and Joel are working for him now."

Father shook his head. "Has he gone to his family for Christmas?"

"I don't think so," said Joel. "He puts the paper out every week now. He can't go away for long."

"Then have him in tomorrow for dinner."

Judith stared at her father.

Joel smiled. "I'll go up later and ask him."

*****

Aunt Alla and Uncle Henry and their children came at noon for Christmas dinner, bringing pies and nuts. Aunt Alla had knitted new mittens for all the children, and gloves for Joel and his father. Ben slipped in just before they sat down to the meal. He chatted pleasantly with the men in the front room while Judith, Aunt Alla, Christina, Lydia, and Molly put the food on the table. The dining room table couldn't hold all the guests, so Joel brought in a dropleaf table from the piazza, and Ned and Bobby sat at it with their cousins, Bert, Frankie, and Hank.

With so many people in the house, Judith managed only a brief moment when she could say to Ben, "Thank you so much. The painting is lovely."

He smiled down at her. "You said at the end of October you missed the leaves."

"Yes, I do." She swallowed. "You've been very kind, and I haven't been able to express my thanks to you. The star—" she faltered, glancing toward it.

"I hoped you wouldn't mind. I told Joel if it didn't seem right to you, that he could—"

"No, it's beautiful. Very different, but wonderful." She looked up at him cautiously, her heart racing. "It wasn't so much the ornament itself, you know."

"Yes, I could see that." He smiled apologetically. "This one's only pasteboard."

She returned his smile. "I shan't break it if I drop it, then."

He stood looking down at her in silence for an instant, contentment touching the corners of his mouth and eyes.

"Dinner was excellent," he said at last. "You are a good hostess, Judith."

He took his leave soon after, and when he was gone, she felt inexplicably bereft. She went over and over their encounter in her mind. *He cares,* she decided. He had complimented her as a woman, as the mistress of the house. That sent a thrill through her, but it opened frightening possibilities. She hadn't allowed herself to admit that she wanted him to think of her that way. Ben Thayer was not looking at her as the oldest child in the Chadbourne family, and she knew that she no longer saw him as an older, somewhat stuffy, slightly mysterious neighbor.

That evening, the family went to Uncle Frank and Aunt Sarah's for supper. The cousins were noisy with mirth. Uncle Peter sat quietly in an armchair. His eyes were bright as he watched the children.

Judith approached him and said cheerily, "Merry Christmas, Uncle Peter. I'm glad to see you so well."

She half expected him to blink at her and quaver, "Who is it?" Instead, he smiled up at her sweetly. "Wesley's oldest gal. What's your name?"

"Judith."

"My mother's name."

She pulled an ottoman close and sat beside him.

"Tell me about your mother, Uncle Peter."

He told her many tales that evening, and soon the other children gathered round to listen, too, until her father announced that it was time to go home. He was heading back to Portsmouth in the morning, and needed a good night's sleep.

\*\*\*\*\*

Dr. Stearns stopped at the print shop the week after Christmas.

"Ed!" Ben exclaimed when he opened the door. "Haven't seen you in weeks."

"Busy season," the doctor replied, stepping inside. "Influenza is going around."

"Come on in the kitchen," Ben urged. "I'm just ready for a cup of coffee."

"Just for a minute. How are you, Ben?" Stearns asked, following him through the parlor and dining room-turned-print shop.

"Healthy as a horse."

"Glad to hear it. I'd say you're a busy man, too. I've been reading your paper. Nice little weekly."

"Thanks." Ben handed him a thick ironstone mug. Ed Stearns had been one of his first subscribers. The doctor sat down at the small maple table in the kitchen, and Ben loaded the stove with firewood.

"I'm here on business," Ed said.

"I told you, I'm healthy."

The doctor smiled. "Not that kind of business. Naomi says it's high time I organized my billing. Can you give me some sort of form? She keeps the ledger for me, but she says I need to write down the amount due every time and put it in the patient's hand. Seems a little crass to me, but Naomi thinks getting paid is important. Can you imagine?"

Ben chuckled. "You've got two children. You need to collect your debts."

"Three soon," Ed murmured.

"What? Three? Congratulations!"

"Thanks." Ed looked around the kitchen, smiling, and raised his eyebrows. "What's this? You got cabin fever and started decorating?"

Ben shrugged. "Just adding a little color to a rather drab house."

"Mrs. Drake wasn't a very imaginative person," Ed noted. "She was a good housekeeper, but all her dresses and her daughters' were cut from the same pattern. Brown for everyday and blue for Sunday. You could count on it. If something was really dull, Naomi would say it was as boring as Etta Drake's wardrobe."

Ben smiled. "Well, I've never been called boring. Tedious, maybe."

Ed snorted and took in Ben's handiwork. "You need a wife." His eyes widened suddenly, and he set down his coffee mug, staring at Ben. "Don't tell me there's a girl behind all this … frippery."

"What makes you say that?" Ben asked and sipped his coffee.

"A woman would appreciate this. Birds. Flowers." Ed eyed him speculatively. "Why don't you just tell me."

Ben opened his mouth, then closed it. He wasn't at all sure of Judith's feelings for him. Ed was a good friend, but he didn't think he could stand having anyone else know about it if she rejected him. So far God and Joel were the only ones who knew how deeply in love he'd fallen. "I don't think so, Ed. Not yet."

"Aha!" Ed pounced on it. "There *is* a woman."

"I didn't say that."

The doctor threw back his head and laughed. "Right. Some men write poetry. Some build a new house or go out and buy a new buggy. You're the man who would paint pictures all over his kitchen."

Ben shrugged and refilled his coffee mug.

# Chapter 15

"Uncle Henry's cutting ice on the river tomorrow," Joel told Judith the second Monday in January. "Ben and I will help him, and he'll pay us in ice."

It was an annual ritual, and the Chadbournes filled their ice house that way. Uncle Henry used to haul sled after sled full of ice to the big ice house in Oakland. From there it would be sold and shipped to cities south of them. Uncle Henry complained lately that the invention of electric refrigerators would spoil the market for ice. But most of their neighbors still used ice boxes and bought their ice from Henry Bickford.

"I didn't suppose Ben would need any ice next year," Judith said, sorting the piles of laundry she needed to wash. "He claims we'll have electricity by Independence Day."

Joel nodded. "He's probably right, but he says he'll help anyway. Do you want me to tell Uncle Henry we don't need any ice?"

"No, we'll need it. Even if we get lights, not everyone on this road can afford a refrigerator."

Joel frowned at her. "Does it bother you that Ben has more money than we do?"

"Of course not. And I'd want you to help Uncle Henry, anyway."

"Judith, if I could, I'd buy you a refrigerator."

She looked hard at him. "I'm not complaining, Joel. And I don't need a refrigerator. We're getting along fine with what we have."

He nodded slowly. "Well, Ben will need ice until the Fourth of July, anyway. It can get hot in June."

"Right." She turned back to her work.

"Things would be a lot easier for you if we had electric power," Joel persisted.

"There are things we need more."

"Like what?"

"Like having Pa home. I don't want him staying away to work so that we can have luxuries."

"Ben says—"

"Ben is different. He doesn't understand our situation."

"How can you say that? Ben grew up on a farm. He knows what it's like."

"Maybe he did once, but he's forgotten. Electricity can't milk cows, Joel."

"Maybe someday it will. And refrigerators can keep milk cold until the dairy picks it up. We wouldn't have to carry it down to the cellar."

"Oh, you're going to put a refrigerator in the barn now?" Judith hated the sarcasm in her voice. "I'm sorry, Joel. I'm just tired." That was a big part of it, she knew. Another big part was that Ben hadn't come around since Christmas, and she had decided he didn't really care, after all. Not about her personally, anyway. He seemed content to spend time with her siblings and crank out the *Hummer*, but he never made any attempt to see her.

She had ruined what sympathy lay between them when she attacked him over the reputation issue. He had apologized, but something had changed between them. Even Christmas Day and his lovely gifts hadn't changed that. He resented her attitude, she was certain now. It made her very sad. Every time she looked at the brilliant maple leaf painting, she felt a stab of grief.

Joel reached into the cookie jar and grabbed two molasses cookies, then retreated out the back door. "Ben knows what he's talking about," he flung at her as the door closed.

\*\*\*\*\*

The ice was thirteen inches thick, and they worked all day in the cold. It was the first time Ben had worked with Henry and Joel, cutting ice. Joel insisted they fill Ben's ice house first.

"I won't need nearly as much as your family will," Ben assured him. "A load or two ought to do it."

When they took a load for the Chadbournes' ice house, Judith came out bundled up in her warm coat.

"Need any help?"

Joel was heaving the blocks into the ice house, and Ben sprinkled shovelfuls of sawdust over and between them.

"How about you bring us some coffee?" Joel panted, setting another block in place.

She turned back toward the house without another word, and Ben leaned on his shovel. "She's not very talkative today, is she?"

"Oh, did you want to talk to her?" Joel winced and shook his head. "You've got to get over this affliction, Ben."

"You think it's hopeless?"

"All I'm saying is, I don't know any two people who have less in common."

Ben laughed. "That can't be true."

"All right, maybe my Aunt Alla has less in common with the Louisiana sergeant who was training us at the army camp than you do with Judith. Maybe."

"Oh, come on. We live on the same road, go to the same church—"

"I'm not talking about that. I'm talking ideas. Judith disagrees with everything you say—no, with everything you *think*."

Ben arched his eyebrows. "That's pretty drastic."

"Trust me, if you think it, she hates it."

"I hoped that maybe she was thawing toward me." Joel scowled.

"Just a little?" Ben pleaded.

"Don't count on it. Every time I mention your name, she bristles."

Judith came from the house carrying a tray with two steaming mugs.

Joel pulled off his gloves, and Ben hopped down off the pile of ice and sawdust.

"Thanks," Joel said, reaching for a cup.

"Thank you, Judith," Ben said, and she nodded at him, not quite meeting his eyes.

"Joel says you're getting a refrigerator," she said after a moment.

Ben looked at her in surprise. "Really?"

Joel shot her a look of annoyance as he blew on his coffee. "I did not say that, Judith. But so what if he does?"

She shrugged. "I must have misunderstood."

"Well, it might be handy, I suppose." Ben sipped his coffee. "Still, one person alone like me…"

"They're putting Uncle Henry out of the ice business. He used to make quite a bit, selling ice every winter." She sounded injured, and Ben eyed her cautiously.

"Told you," said Joel.

"What?" Judith glared at him.

"Nothing."

She looked suspiciously from her brother to Ben and back. "What are you talking about?"

"Ice," said Joel.

She all but stamped her foot. Ben held back the laughter that wanted to burst out from his chest. He didn't blame her for being cross with Joel. She wouldn't see the humor in the situation, though.

She turned her glare on him, and he took a quick sip of coffee. "That's very good coffee," he said.

"No, it's not."

Joel hooted in glee. "You see? You see what I mean, Ben?"

"What is wrong with you?" Judith's eyes were flashing now. "Father said when he was home that it's terrible. He said it's the worst coffee we've had all through the war. But I couldn't see just throwing it out."

Ben smiled. "It's fine."

She looked at him, then at Joel. He thought for an instant that she would cry. Instead, she turned and marched toward the house.

*****

"Where's Ben?" she couldn't help asking, when Joel brought the next load alone.

"He took Uncle Henry's sled full to the Sibleys."

She looked up at him apprehensively. "Is he angry?"

Joel just laughed, and she looked away, trying to squelch her disappointment.

"I'm surprised he could take a day off," she mused. "He's been helping you in the woods and getting the paper out, too."

"He made some sketches at the pond this morning," Joel confided.

"For the paper?"

"Yes. He says someday the *Hummer* will have photographs, but for now, his engravings will have to do."

She hesitated, watching cautiously as he worked. It was cold, and she had work to do. She couldn't stand there all day. At last she asked, "Why were you two carrying on so about the coffee?"

"Oh, Judith, it wasn't the coffee. It was your attitude."

She went back to the kitchen. Was it so terrible to wish they had better coffee? Joel was immature, and she could put up with his nonsense occasionally, but it hurt that Ben seemed to think she was unreasonable.

She spent most of her winter days alone. Snow fell at intervals, piling higher and higher. The boys riddled the drifts with caves and passageways. The ox-drawn snowplows and rollers inched through from the Oakland line to the Augusta boundary.

When the heavy snowfall put an end to the ice harvesting, Joel resumed driving the children to school. They left in the sleigh each morning, alternating Lady and Chub in harness. Judith went about her housework, caught up the mending, and found time to sew a new dress for Christina.

On Fridays, Saturdays, and Mondays, Joel spent the day at Ben's house or on the road selling advertising for the *Hummer*.

He was learning the printing and publishing trade, and Judith saw that he was content with it.

*****

Christina's writing skills improved, and Ben couldn't help feeling paternal pride in her. At church on Sunday, folks would tell her they could hardly wait to read her stories the next day.

"This young lady's going to be a famous reporter," old Mrs. Grafton told Ben after the service in mid-January, loudly enough so Christina was sure to hear.

"Could be," said Ben.

Christina's laugh rippled out, and she beamed on Mrs. Grafton. "I'm not sure what I want to do yet. But I'm planning to go to college."

"College?" Mrs. Grafton drew back to appraise her through her spectacles. "The teacher's college?"

"I don't know yet," Christina replied happily. "Judith says if I work hard, I can go wherever I want. I'm sort of interested in medicine."

"Oh, you want to be a nurse," Mrs. Grafton nodded.

"Nurse?" scoffed Ed Stearns, who stood behind her in the aisle and had overheard the entire conversation. "This young lady could be a doctor."

"A lady doctor?" Mrs. Sutton piped up. "That's a novel idea."

"Not so novel in the civilized world," said Stearns. "She's smart as a whip, and there are schools that will take women now. Are you truly interested in medicine, Miss Chadbourne?"

"Well, I think I am," Christina replied, blushing, a bit overwhelmed by the attention. "I had thought about nursing."

"She's a writer," Mrs. Grafton contradicted.

"Rot," said Stearns. He took his wife's arm and turned toward the door, but looked back to tell Christina, "You stop by my office after school tomorrow, young lady. I've got some new equipment you may want to tell your readers about. And

I'll give you the names of some colleges where you could prepare for medical school."

Ben waited outside the church for a hasty conference with his star reporter.

"I want you to interview Hal Richardson this week," he said, as he walked with Christina toward the Chadbournes' wagon. "I saw him at the post office yesterday. He spent three months in western France, and he tells a good yarn. I'll put some art with it, after I see your story."

Christina nodded soberly. "I'll see about it tomorrow."

"Any word from your father on when he'll be home?"

"Not yet," she replied. "Say, Ben, are we going to run a story on that draft dodger, Bergdoll? They're still looking for him. I heard he visited his mother, and they still couldn't catch him."

"Local news only, Scoop. Leave that to the dailies and the wire services."

Christina frowned. "But it's really interesting. People are asking me if I've heard anything. They want to know what's up."

"Hal Richardson will give you plenty of exciting copy, kiddo. What do you think I'm going to do, send you to Philadelphia to interview Bergdoll's mother?"

"I suppose not," she said with a grimace. "All right, Hal Richardson it is."

"Right. If you hear about any slackers in Sidney, I might consider giving you free reign. Are you really interested in medicine?" Ben asked, looking around to see if there was a chance he could get a word with Judith. He was too late. Joel was already giving her a hand as she entered the sleigh to sit next to Bobby.

"I don't really know what I want to do," Christina laughed. "I like writing, but nursing seems nobler, somehow. Until this year, I always figured I'd be a teacher, or just ... you know, a farmer's wife."

"Well, that's not so bad," Ben said vaguely. Judith looked his way, and he tipped his hat. She nodded soberly, and he wondered just where he stood with her now. It was very unsatisfactory, seeing her across the church and getting secondhand reports from Joel, mostly negative ones at that. Maybe Joel was right, and Judith had no interest in him. "You haven't got any particular farmer in mind, have you?"

Christina smiled sadly. "All the best boys are gone now, Mr. Thayer."

"Come on, Chris," Joel called. "Don't make Chub stand in the cold."

She hurried to the back of the sleigh and climbed in with Ned and Lydia. Joel put his foot on the step.

"See you this evening, Ben."

"Yes, and I'll need you directly after chores tomorrow morning to help me get the *Hummer* delivered." His peaceful agrarian life had become a whirlwind of responsibility. He watched Judith tuck a wool lap robe over Bobby's knees and wondered if she was avoiding looking at him again.

"Sure." Joel glanced toward the children, then leaned toward Ben and said softly, "Chris always adored Harry, you know."

"Ah." The whole town had turned out for Harry's funeral at the end of November, giving the boy a hero's sendoff. Christina had bawled without restraint, he remembered, but then, all the women had cried. He'd shed a few tears himself. He sighed. She was young to bear that kind of sorrow, but on the other hand, she was young enough to be resilient.

He waved to the children as Joel urged Chub into a trot and the sleigh pulled out of the church yard. There was too much grief to go around these days. Just when his own seemed to be easing a bit, those he loved were weighed down by it. Despite Judith's coolness, his desire to uplift the family at River Rest was stronger than ever.

*****

On the days when he didn't work for Ben, Joel cut firewood and dragged it out of the woods with the team of oxen. Judith was certain Ben helped him frequently, but he never came to the house with Joel, and her brother never spoke of it.

The piles of logs grew in the barnyard, and Judith began to feel that the Chadbournes were going to be all right. A big woodpile meant a warm house next winter. Between her and Joel, they could conquer the shadows of hunger and cold. She never stopped thanking God for bringing Joel home.

She startled herself one bright afternoon at the end of January by singing as she fed wet clothes through the wringer. Not the catchy songs Joel sang. The family was behind the times and didn't have a radio, but her brother had brought a few popular tunes back with him from Lewiston, "Oh, How I Hate to Get Up in the Morning," and "There's a Long, Long Trail Awinding." But Judith chose a stirring hymn, "My faith has found a resting place, not in device or creed. I trust the ever-living one—for me His wounds shall plead."

Her hands were red and chapped from scrubbing the clothes in the tub of warm wash water and harsh soap, and her arms ached from cranking the handle on the wringer, but she rejoiced as the clean shirts and towels and socks squeezed on through and fell, flat and misshapen, into the tub of rinse water on the other side of the collapsible wringer frame. After she had swished them thoroughly in that, they went through the wringer again, into the big ash-splint basket.

She pulled on her cape and gloves and dragged the basket out the back door to the clothesline. Laundry was always a tedious chore, but in the frigid months it was especially arduous. Her gloves didn't do much good, as they soon soaked through, and she could barely hold the wooden clothespins with her icy fingers. She hummed on determinedly, refusing to let winter and loss get the better of her.

*A resting place*, she prayed silently. Her thoughts became a conversation with God as she worked. *This farm will never be that for a body, but a heart can find peace anyplace, can't it, Lord?* She heard no reply, but she didn't expect one. God's answers to her mute pleas came through His written word, early in the morning over tea, or after sunset, when the children were tucked in bed and her mending was laid aside.

*Maybe that's what Mother was thinking when she chose the farm's name*, she thought with a start. *Spiritual rest.* She stared off down the pasture to the frozen river. Her mother was always serene, though her hands were never idle. She never showed the turmoil and worry that Judith felt so often.

She carried her empty basket inside and warmed her hands at the stove, then made tea in her mother's china teapot. It had a small chip in the spout, but Judith loved it. It had been a wedding present, she knew. The lilacs on the rounded side always cheered her in winter.

The back door opened, and she heard Joel tramp into the kitchen.

"Take your boots off," she called without thinking.

"Want me to dump this wash water?" he asked.

"Oh, yes, thank you."

"Well, I have to keep my boots on, then."

"Sorry," she said. "Go ahead. I'll wipe the floor after you."

He picked up the first tub and strained as he carried it toward the back door. Judith dashed to open the door wide for him.

"Have a cup of tea with me?" she asked.

"Got any doughnuts?"

"No, but sugar cookies and hermits."

Joel grunted, and she took that for a yes. He tipped the tub and dumped the dirty water in the side yard, then came back for the other tub. Judith got a mug from the cupboard for him and put cookies on a plate. He came back in and wiped his boots on the mat, then sat down to remove them while she got the rag mop from the cellarway and mopped the wet floor.

They sat down in the dining room together. It was a rare thing for her brother to relax with her during the day now. When they were younger, they would often play together and read or study in the evening, but now it seemed they were always too busy.

"So, you like what you're doing for Mr. Thayer?" she asked, filling his mug.

He shrugged. "I'm not crazy about the part where I go around and try to sell advertisements. But he needs that, so I do it. He says he'll teach me to drive his car this summer. That will be worth it! And I like working on the press."

His eyes gleamed, and Judith said, "You like machinery, don't you?"

"Don't you?"

She smiled. "I like what it can do, but I'm not wild about taking everything apart, the way you seem to be. Joel, have you thought about what you want to do with your life? I mean, do you want to keep on here at the farm, and milk cows all the time?"

"I don't know."

"But you like working for Ben. Not just working with him, I mean, but you like the printing part. The machinery."

"Know what I think the farm needs?"

"What?"

"A tractor," Joel said with shining eyes. "Ben showed me a picture of one in an agriculture magazine. In a few years, all the farms will have their own tractors."

"What for?" Judith asked in surprise.

"Everything. Haying, planting, harvesting, hauling wood. Just everything."

"Wouldn't they pack the soil down?" she asked doubtfully.

"Maybe some," Joel conceded, "but the time you'd save would be worth it."

"They'll be expensive."

"Ben says I could make one."

Judith shook her head. "Another of Ben's ideas."

"What have you got against Ben?" Joel asked with a note of defensiveness.

"Nothing," she said in surprise. "Why do you say that?"

"You avoid him, and you treat him coldly. He's my friend, Judith. I like him a lot. And he likes you."

Judith tried to keep her face serene, though her pulse raced. "I like him. I just don't know him very well."

"You've known him more than three years," Joel protested.

"Not well. You know we didn't neighbor much with him until recently."

Joel shook his head, exasperated. "What is it that you need to know?"

She shrugged. His intensity made her feel he was asking out of something deeper than curiosity, and she tried to put into words what she wanted to know about Ben Thayer, the thing that would make her feel completely at ease with him. How could you say to your brother, *I want to know what's in his heart?*

She said softly, "What really made him come here, I suppose. He told me he'd had enough of New York, and just up and left the city, but I felt there was more to it."

Her brother studied her gravely. Judith loved Joel deeply, but his pensive frown was making her uncomfortable.

"You're right, there's more to it," Joel said at last. "Why don't you ask him?"

"I did, the day we went to see you in Lewiston. He didn't tell me." She recalled how he had brushed off her question about his past, why he had left his well-paying job in New York. He had most certainly avoided talking about it.

"Maybe if you asked him again now ..."

She shook her head uneasily. "If he wants me to know, he'll tell me. No, Joel. He doesn't want to talk to me about things like that."

"You haven't tried."

She sighed. "I don't think I want to."

Joel's eyes narrowed, but she sat silent. It was too painful to think that Ben might rebuff her again if she probed into his past. This uneasy friendship was perhaps marginally better than open rejection.

# Chapter 16

Ben was awakened Sunday morning in the gray hour before dawn by a frantic hammering on his piazza door. He rolled out of bed quickly, ran to the window, and threw it open.

"Hey!" He shouted. "What's going on?"

A man stepped back from his front steps and looked up at him. "The Grange Hall's burning. I'm trying to raise some manpower to keep it from spreading to the sheds and over to the church."

Ben thought he recognized Bart Howland, the oldest son of one of the selectmen. "I'll be right there! Have you been to Chadbournes'?"

"My next stop."

He hurriedly pulled on his trousers and socks. There had been a supper at the Grange last night, he knew. Christina had put notice of it in last week's *Hummer*. And those flimsy horse sheds between the Grange Hall and the church were so much tinder.

\*\*\*\*\*

"I'm going!" Christina cried. She had rushed into the hallway with Judith when Bart Howland pounded on the door. Joel was already up for morning chores, pulling on his boots in the entry, and the girls could hear their brief conversation from the upstairs landing.

"No!" Judith pulled her robe close around her in the chill. "Ben will get the story."

"They'll need Ben to help with the fire." Christina headed back toward the room she shared with Lydia. "I'll be safe and stay out of the way, Judith. Joel will be there. Besides, if I get the story, Ben will have time to draw pictures to illustrate it."

"I'm not waiting for you," Joel yelled up the stairway, and Judith heard the back door slam.

"All right." She followed Christina into her room and tried to remain calm. "Joel will take Chub, I'm sure. You take Lady, and go slow. We can't have you getting tossed in a snowbank and breaking your neck."

"I'll be careful," Christina promised, pulling her nightgown off in the half light and dropping it to the floor.

Judith turned away while her sister dressed. "You come back later, and I'll have coffee and doughnuts ready in the sleigh. You can take it over for the men."

"I might not have time," Christina replied. "Better run over to Suttons' and ask them to take it." She put on her oldest house dress and plopped down on the edge of the bed to pull on her high boots. Lydia stirred and sat up.

"What's happening?" she asked sleepily.

"The Grange is burning," Christina replied tersely. "I'm going over."

"I'd better get the boys up to feed the stock," Judith said wearily.

Ned and Bobby, whose bedroom was on the back of the house, had slept through the clamor, and Judith had to shake them awake.

"Will they have church this morning?" Bobby asked, yawning, when Judith had given them the news.

"Not if the church burns." Ned was already half dressed. "Wish Joel took me."

"He didn't have time to stop for you," Judith said. "I'm going down and start cooking. You boys go to the barn with Lydia and milk and feed the stock."

"Yes'm," said Ned. "Can I go to the fire after?"

"You most certainly may not."

Ned scowled and padded down the stairs behind her, buttoning his shirt. At the back door he thrust his feet into his boots and pulled on his barn frock. "I could take Lady," he wheedled.

"Christina has Lady, and I'm not letting you walk that far. It's below freezing."

"When I'm big, I'm going to work for Mr. Thayer, and then I'll get to go to all the fun stuff," he muttered.

Two hours later the chores were done and the children were scrubbed, dressed, and fed, ready for Sunday school, but they had no way to get there. Mrs. Sutton had come for Judith's jug of coffee and basket of doughnuts and muffins, adding it to a supply she had prepared, and gone on to the Grange Hall with the refreshments for the firefighters.

Judith and Lydia sat tensely on the sofa, waiting for news. Ned lounged on the carpet, reading a book, and Bobby was holding Sass, the black and white kitten that Judith had allowed him to adopt from among a litter of barn cats.

"If someone comes by, we can ride with them," Lydia suggested timidly.

"I don't know as there will be services, after all," Judith replied. She stood up and looked out the front window toward the road. "Perhaps we should have our own Sunday school today. I have a feeling we won't be getting to church."

She led them in prayer for the firefighters, and each one pleaded that the church be spared.

It was nearly noon when Ben, Joel, and Christina rode back together, tired and filthy. Judith and the children ran out into the dooryard to meet them.

"Did the church go?" Lydia asked fearfully.

Joel's grimy face was weary. "No, but it was a near thing."

"The Grange hall burned flat, and the horse sheds are gone." Christina had more vim than the two men could muster. "When the sheds started going, they knocked down the ones nearest the church and pulled the wood away. Dozens of people turned out to haul water. They chopped holes in the river ice and soaked blankets and brought buckets and barrels of water up in wagons."

"What started it?" Ned asked eagerly.

"Not sure," Christina replied. "They had the stoves going last night for the supper. They thought they'd shut things down, but could be it started as a chimney fire, after everyone left."

"I can see you'll have quite a story to write for next week's paper," Judith said sadly.

"Next week? Forget it! We're breaking this story. Right, Mr. Thayer?" Christina swiveled in the saddle to look at Ben.

"Right, Scoop. Can't let it wait a week."

"But don't you have the *Hummer* all laid out for printing?" Judith asked.

"We'll add an extra page, an insert," Ben explained. "If Christina can write it up today—" He broke off, eyeing her with hesitation. "That is, if you don't mind. I don't usually work on Sunday, but this is a rare thing."

Judith nodded. "The Waterville paper will pick it up."

"Yes, and we want to be first."

"I don't see why she can't work on it this afternoon," Judith decided. "Will you stay to dinner, Mr. Thayer?"

"Some of the ladies brought food to the fire." He gestured toward his soot-blackened clothing. "No offense, but I think I'll head home for a bath and a nap."

Christina spent the entire afternoon laboring over her account of the fire. She had buttonholed the fire chief, the Master of the Grange, and several other prominent citizens for quotes for her story. She had also talked to the minister, and was able to prepare copy Ben could include in a sidebar, assuring the parishioners that the church had survived with some blistered paint on the side nearest the Grange Hall, and services would go on uninterrupted.

Judith was shocked that night when they drove over in the sleigh for the evening service. The stench of burnt wood hung heavily in the air, and the smoldering pile of rubble where the Grange Hall had been was a stark reminder of the transience of things on earth. She felt a great thankfulness as she turned her gaze to the little white church that stood solitary now, unencumbered by the sheds that had spread out between it and the Grange. The steeple seemed taller and straighter than before, against the star-lit sky.

"Makes you grateful, doesn't it?"

She turned to find Ben beside her.

"Yes. Yes, it does. I didn't expect to see you here tonight, Mr. Thayer."

"Ah, well, the soul needs rest and refreshment."

"Yes."

He nodded and walked away, toward Dr. Stearns, who was looking about in confusion, searching for something he could tie his horse to. Judith watched him bleakly. Did she imagine that he had avoided her since the confrontation in her parlor over Christina's behavior? He was still courteous, but seemed aloof somehow. She had done that. Her heart ached. Somehow she had set their friendship back several furlongs. His eyes didn't sparkle anymore when he saw her; they just looked sad. At Christmas her hope had risen, but since then he'd seemed more cautious, more subdued, and simply more absent.

He used to come down to see Joel. Now Joel was up there several days a week. He had come around with offers of neighborly assistance before, but now her brother was home to take care of the things Ben might have done. She didn't want to believe he'd never cared for her. It had been such a wondrous feeling, one she had hardly dared accept, but once she had, she knew she never wanted to do without it again.

She looked back toward the ruins of the Grange Hall. A thin plume of smoke oozed out from the charred remains and wafted skyward.

"You all right, Judith?"

She jumped. "Oh, Joel. You startled me."

"Sort of mournful, isn't it?" He nodded toward the debris. "I mean, besides the expense and the work to rebuild it. Part of history is gone."

She nodded. "Was it insured?"

"Chris says yes. But still ..."

"Is Ben avoiding me?" she asked abruptly, turning to face him.

Joel's eyes flared in surprise. "Would you blame him? You haven't given him much encouragement."

"Encouragement?" She felt her cheeks redden. "He's never hinted that he wanted any."

"Hasn't he?" Joel sounded genuinely surprised. "Taking you to Lewiston, that painting he made you at Christmas, and the star for the tree. Not to mention he caved in to you on keeping Christina away from the house."

Judith swallowed. "Those were just ..." Her voice faded. They weren't *just* anything. He did care, or at least, he *had* cared. "Have I offended him?" she asked at last.

"I wouldn't say that. But he may be close to giving up hope."

She gasped. "Joel, I didn't know he was hoping."

"You didn't?" He shook his head. "I always thought you were the smart one of the family, Judith. Ben is a good man. I can't understand why you hold him off the way you do."

"I—I do that?"

"He kept asking me if I thought you'd come around to liking him better, but I had to tell him I couldn't see it."

Judith felt a wrenching pain vying inside her with an urge to strangle Joel. "You—you told him that? And he cares about me after all this time?"

"Look at him."

She glanced furtively to where Ben stood with Dr. and Mrs. Stearns, deep in conversation.

"What am I supposed to see?"

"Keep looking."

She followed Joel's instructions, though it pained her to watch Ben for long. Yes, she had come to care very deeply about him. She knew that now.

His eyes flickered toward them and caught hers for an instant, with a haunting, wistful look. He turned back to Ed Stearns, and Judith exhaled, realizing suddenly that she had held her breath.

Joel said in her ear, "He can't keep his eyes off you. That's why he sits ahead of us in church. He told me he'd just stare at you the whole time and not hear a word of the sermon if he sat behind us."

She took an unsteady breath and looked around for the children. "We ought to go in."

"I'll get the kids." Ned had organized a game of tag with several other children, and they were climbing on the pile of lumber that had been salvaged from the horse sheds. Joel strode toward them.

Judith glanced back toward Ben. He and the Stearnses were moving toward the church steps. Before they reached them, Ben looked back over his shoulder at her, and she felt another stab of longing as his eyes met hers. She tried to smile, but she was suddenly afraid she was about to cry. Ben nodded gravely and followed Dr. Stearns up the steps.

# Chapter 17

The week after the fire dragged by, and Judith tried to escape her loneliness by working harder than ever. For everyone else, it was business as usual, school and work and visiting friends, but she felt she had brought a bleak isolation on herself. She hadn't seen Ben, even from a distance. She had caught herself at breakfast, waiting for Christina or Joel to mention his name. She even toyed with making an excuse to see him, but rejected that idea. The last time she'd tried to discuss a sensitive point with Ben, she'd wound up hurt and remorseful.

*Lord, you know all about this, and if you want it straightened out, I'm sure you can do it much better than I ever could.* Her initial anger with Joel mellowed into acceptance, and willed herself not to fret over Ben's perception of her, colored by her brother's viewpoint.

Late on Friday afternoon she let the three younger children go out to the pasture after school with their sleds, while she tackled a huge basket of clothes that needed ironing. Joel was still at Ben's, setting type for the *Hummer,* and Christina was conducting an interview in the front room.

Judith had allowed Christina to use their mother's desk, and she was deep in conversation with Andrew Warren, the oldest boy from a family of ten children across Snow Pond, in Belgrade. At Ben's request, he had come across the frozen lake so Christina could get his story. Andrew was directing his siblings and a few of their cousins and friends in an impromptu drama troupe. They were presenting a melodrama, *My Awful Dad,* the last week in February, and the public was invited to attend.

The bits of conversation Judith overheard made her smile. Andrew seemed to be a young fellow who enjoyed life. Judith's impression of the Warren family was that of a group of creative young people with long evenings on their hands. They had exchanged boredom for theatrics, and expected to give the community an evening to remember. The handsome director had presented Christina with complementary tickets, and Judith wondered if her sister wasn't smitten with him. Christina might even decide to try acting next.

After taking them a plate of cookies, Judith exchanged her cooling flatiron for a hot one off the stove. As she smoothed the stubborn wrinkles from the boys' cotton shirts, she planned what she would do with the yarn Aunt Sarah had brought her the day before. Ned needed new socks, that was certain, and Joel had already worn through the gloves he'd received at Christmas. She wasn't expert yet at knitting fingers, and she wondered if mittens wouldn't be just as good. No, she was fooling herself. A man needed gloves. She would have to ask one of her aunts to help her master the technique.

She thought she would knit a pair of socks for Uncle Peter as well. She wasn't sure if he would go back to his little cabin in the spring, but she wanted to be sure he was warm if he did.

She heard a horse galloping down the road and stepped quickly to the dining room doorway. Through the window she saw Joel on Ben's gelding.

"Judith!" he yelled, pulling Chester in at the driveway. Christina appeared in the parlor doorway, open-mouthed, with Andrew right behind her. As Judith ran to the front door, the two young people followed.

"Ben shut his hand in the press," Joel called without dismounting. "I have to get Dr. Stearns."

"Is it bad?"

"Pretty bad."

"Should I go up there?" she asked.

"Wouldn't hurt."

Joel was off again, kicking Chester into a run.

Judith pushed past Christina and Andrew, hurrying to get her coat.

"Is there anything I can do, Miss Chadbourne?" Andrew asked anxiously.

"No, thank you, Mr. Warren."

"Let me come with you," Christina pleaded.

"No. You stay here with Lydia and the boys."

Judith saw the disappointment in her eyes, but Christina didn't argue, and for that she was grateful.

"I suppose I should be going," Andrew said, looking wistfully at Christina.

"I believe I have all the information I need," Christina replied, clearly distracted. "Or perhaps you would step out to the pasture with me. I ought to call the other children in, in case Judith needs one of the boys to run an errand."

Judith saw Andrew's contented expression as she dashed past them, and knew he would stay with Christina and the children until she returned. She ran, gasping, up the road and turned in at Ben's. The driveway had never seemed so long.

She pounded on the door, but didn't wait for an answer, throwing it open and charging into the parlor.

"Mr. Thayer!"

He was sitting on the couch, holding a dish towel tightly to his left hand. Blood had soaked through the linen towel. Terrified, Judith went to her knees beside him.

"Are you all right?" she asked.

He smiled as if he were very tired. "I'll make it, I think, if Ed Stearns is home."

"What can I do?"

"Ice, maybe, and another cloth?"

She hurried through the print shop to the kitchen and looked around. Where would he keep towels?

She caught her breath. Each cabinet door was painted with a scene of familiar birds. Robins on one, chickadees, purple martins, grosbeaks, phoebes, lifelike and beautiful. On a tall cupboard in the corner, her bird feeder was painted, and the raucous blue jay was in possession.

She forced her concentration back to the moment and strode to the oak icebox built into the outside wall. In the largest compartment was a block of ice. She found a small ice pick nearby and chipped away until she had a pile of small pieces.

She opened drawers wildly until she found clean dish towels, and pulled out two. Wrapping the ice in one, she ran back to the parlor. Ben was leaning back against the cushions with a look of great patience, his skin pale.

"Here." She sat down beside him and held out the towel with the ice.

He stirred and looked at her. "I don't think I ought to take this one off." He took the ice from her with his right hand and grimaced as he held it to the bloody towel that covered his left.

She held out the other clean towel and said, "Here, put this under it." He let her lay it over his knee, then rested his hands on it.

"I'm so sorry." She felt useless. If only they had telephones. "Is it painful?"

"Just a wee bit." His face was gray.

"Joel will get the doctor."

"I hope so."

"What should we do if he can't find him?"

"I don't suppose you ever drove an automobile?"

She shook her head bleakly.

"Well, I about took the end of my fourth finger off, and the middle finger's smashed pretty badly. We'll just hope Ed's home."

She sat by him helplessly for a minute. "Is there anything else I can do?"

"Check the stove," he said, gritting his teeth. "Make sure the teakettle's full."

She went back to the kitchen and lifted the lid of the wood burner. Coals were glowing in the bottom of the firebox. She bent to get a stick of wood and smiled in spite of herself. Kittens were painted on the front of the wood box. Rolling, pouncing, stalking kittens. She quickly put three logs into the firebox and closed it, then lifted the teakettle. Half full.

She took it to the cast iron sink. A pitcher of water sat on the drainboard, and she poured half down the little pitcher pump at the edge of the sink to prime it, then pumped the handle furiously. It was slack at first, but soon grabbed and resisted her efforts. Water splashed out, and she held the teakettle under the flow as she continued to pump with her right hand.

The water overflowed the top of the kettle as she stared at the splashboard behind the sink. A rural scene went the length of it. Willow trees, a winding lane, a horse and open buggy. Beside the lane ran a stream, and a barefoot boy sat on a rock, fishing. A bridge crossed the stream farther along, where a girl leaned on its railing.

She splashed a little water from the overfilled kettle, put the cover on, set it on the stove, and hurried back to Ben.

He was leaning back on the couch with his eyes closed. She sat down hesitantly and put her hand on his shoulder.

"Ben?" she whispered.

He opened his eyes and smiled a little. "See? You can say it."

She smiled back. "Are you all right?"

"I'm not sure. Felt a little woozy."

She touched the ice pack delicately, but he winced, and she took her hand away.

"He'll be here soon," she promised.

"It's getting numb."

"That's good." There was blood on the sleeve of his machine-made, pale blue shirt. She would take it when this was over and wash it in cold water, along with the soiled towels. The shirt was made of better quality cloth than those Joel and Father wore on Sunday, although Ben had been wearing it while doing his messy printing. She supposed Ben didn't worry about getting ink on his shirts. He probably ordered them by the dozen from Portland or New York. If he couldn't get the stains out, he'd throw them away.

He inhaled deeply, and she tried to think of something she could say to distract him. "What were you printing today? Not the *Hummer*."

"No, it was handbills for the play. *My Awful Dad.* It should be funny. Want to go? The ice is so thick, you can cross the lake with teams now. Be there in half an hour."

She smiled. He hadn't lost his spirit. "Andrew's down at the house."

"He brought me the text on his way over."

"He's a nice boy."

Ben closed his eyes again, and she watched him, wondering how much pain he was in. "What happened, Ben?"

"I was careless, that's all. Hurrying. I had things set up in the press, and I pushed the cover down. Hard." He shook his head. "But I forgot to tell my hand to move."

Judith looked at the wad of towels around his hand. Blood had come through the second towel. She couldn't tell if it was still spreading.

"The birds…" she said softly.

"What birds?" His eyelids flew up.

"In the kitchen." She felt a flush spreading upward from her collar.

"What kind of birds?" he asked in confusion.

"All kinds. On the cupboards."

"Oh." He closed his eyes again.

"They took me by surprise."

He didn't say anything, and she thought he was asleep, or unconscious. Carefully, she put her hand up to his brow. His hair was damp, and beads of sweat stood on his forehead, but his skin was cool. His eyes remained closed.

"Are you all right, Ben?" she said close to his ear, afraid he was losing consciousness.

"No. I love you, Judith."

Her stomach lurched. She sat up straight and stared at him, unable to respond.

Slowly his eyes came open.

"I'm not delirious," he said.

His eyes searched hers for a long instant. All the admonishments Joel had given her in the past few weeks whirled through her mind. What was the proper thing to say at a time like this, if you wanted a man to know that you cared deeply, but didn't want to seem forward? Perhaps there was no proper thing. Perhaps it wasn't the time to be proper at all.

She drew a shaky breath. Christina would know exactly what to say, and that knowledge irritated her.

"Ben, I—"

"What?"

"If Joel led you to believe I was angry with you, or—" He was watching her intently. "Well, I'm not. And I'm very sorry that I've treated you badly. That wasn't my intention at all. I just didn't know how to—" She broke off helplessly. *He loves me! Thank you, Lord!*

The sound of an engine came from outside, and Judith jumped up, unsure if she was more relieved or disappointed. Dr. Stearns and Joel hurried into the house.

"Benjamin, what have you been up to?" Dr. Stearns said loudly as he entered the parlor.

Ben sat up and held out his hands. Joel got a straight chair for Dr. Stearns, and he sat down facing Ben and began unwrapping the towels.

"Ice is good," he said. "Fingers severed?"

"Not quite, I think," said Ben. He jumped and grimaced as the doctor removed the wrappings, and blood oozed from the wounds.

"Nasty," said Dr. Stearns.

Judith felt queasy and turned her head away.

"I'd like to take you to the hospital," said the doctor.

"Thanks just the same, Ed," Ben said companionably.

"You imbecile," the doctor replied with affection. "You need surgery."

"So do it."

Dr. Stearns sighed. "You've lost a lot of blood."

"Losing more every second. Stitch me up, Ed."

The doctor shook his head. "We'd better get you upstairs. I'll need to give you chloroform. Don't want you passing out on the floor." He put the ice back against the wound and Ben drew his breath in sharply.

"Got hot water?" the doctor asked, looking at Judith for the first time.

"Yes, a teakettle full."

"Heat some more. Rinse a wash basin with boiling water and bring it to me upstairs, and the kettle of water." He turned back to the patient. "Ready, Ben?"

Joel stepped in close to Ben, and Ben put his right hand on his friend's shoulder and heaved himself to his feet. Judith went to the kitchen and rummaged for a basin. She hesitated at the bottom of the stairs. She had never been upstairs in the house, and felt she was intruding. She thought how she would feel if unexpected company insisted on a tour of the Chadbournes' upstairs. Surely a bachelor would balk at having his privacy violated.

But the doctor needed the things quickly. She took a deep breath and started up the steps. Almost immediately, she knew something was odd about that stairway. By the halfway point, her heart was racing as what she saw sank in.

Above her, Dr. Stearns was talking, and Ben was answering irascibly, but she couldn't make out their words. In the dim light on the stairway, she *could* make out plants. On the riser of each step, grasses and vines were painted. The higher she went, the more detailed the paintings became. The third step had ferns, the fourth mushrooms, the fifth clover, and on up, through buttercups, daisies, and sweet peas. The riser of the top step was a riot of wild roses.

She stopped before she reached it, just looking, then slowly turned her eyes to the walls. On each side of the stairs, a large scene was painted on the wall. On her right, a schooner under full sail headed for the open sea. On her left was an apple tree, heavy with ripe fruit. Two boys scrambled among the branches, while a moody Hereford steer loitered below. She squinted at the boys and smiled in wonder. They were unmistakably Ned and Bobby.

She roused herself and hurried up the last few steps and into the bedroom. Ben lay on the bed, against white pillow slips. The high maple headboard stood against one wall. Joel was on the far side, pulling back the curtains at the two windows that faced the river and fastening them with tiebacks. The doctor had hastily cleared a washstand and was setting out his instruments.

Dr. Stearns looked from Joel to Judith. "I'll need an assistant."

"I'll do it," Joel said.

Judith was relieved. She thought she could have done it if she had to, but she would much rather not. She eased into a corner and watched, praying silently. When she couldn't watch, she turned toward the window.

There on a low bench, tubes of paint lay in a disorderly row. A can of liquid held several brushes. Her eyes traveled slowly along to the end wall of the room, and she gasped. Painted on the wall was the beginning of a lush English garden. A white slatted gate was invitingly open, and beyond it a dozen varieties of flowers thrived on the plaster wall that had been washed in cerulean. Puffy clouds studded the brilliant sky, and sparrows perched in the branches of a blooming French lilac. She held her breath, then smiled tremulously as she spotted a toad peering at her from under a bleeding heart plant. A path of paving stones led to the corner of the wall and around it toward her. Ivy snaked up the edge of the window. The garden was obviously meant to continue.

"Relax, now, Benjamin," said Dr. Stearns. "Joel, hold this for me, just like that."

Judith tiptoed quietly from the room and drifted slowly down the stairs, looking around at the paintings, taking in details she hadn't noticed before. She tried to rein in her chaotic emotions, as her anxiety for Ben mingled with her wonder at the gorgeous scenes unfolding before her.

Even the back of the door at the bottom of the stairs had been embellished, and she felt tears well in her eyes as she looked at the winter scene, with a couple riding over a snow-covered field in a sleigh. The horse looked suspiciously like Chub. *That could be Mother and Father*, she thought. Yes, the barn in the distance was the dairy barn at River Rest.

She sat in the parlor downstairs, praying. *Lord, I'm overwhelmed, and I don't know what to say. Please help Dr. Stearns now. You know what's best.* A calm swept over her as she prayed for Ben, trusting God to control the situation. She kept on praying, and slowly she knew that she had found peace at last, trusting that God would do what was the absolute best for Ben and all of them.

# Chapter 18

Joel stayed the night at Ben's house, and Judith got up in the darkness to prepare breakfast for both households. When she had shooed Ned, Christina and Lydia to the barn to do chores, she walked up the road with a basket containing fresh eggs, bacon, warm biscuits, and a jar of applesauce for Ben and Joel's breakfast.

Joel met her at the door in his stocking feet. "Hi. I'm just going out to feed Chester."

"How is Ben?"

"Still sleeping."

She took over the kitchen without a second thought. She felt at home here now. The stove lid clattered cozily when she fed the fire, and the river scene behind the sink cheered her as she filled the teakettle. She hugged to herself his declaration of love. It was a glorious thought, but what if he regretted blurting it out in his pain?

She laid a place for Joel at the tiny kitchen table and meticulously prepared a tray for Ben. She found the ironstone mug she had seen earlier in the print shop, and when the coffee was ready she poured it full and carried the tray carefully up the stairs, pausing outside his bedroom door.

"Ben?" she called softly.

There was a stirring and a creaking within.

"Yes?"

"Breakfast. May I come in?"

"What? Room service?"

She entered smiling. "Did I wake you?"

"No. I was lying here thinking I ought to feed Chester, and then I smelled coffee and remembered Joel was here. I was just being lazy, not wanting to move."

"You're not supposed to move. Stay in bed this morning. Dr. Stearns will come by later."

"You didn't have to come." His intense blue eyes watched her as she set the tray down on the dresser and came to arrange his pillows so he could sit up comfortably.

"I don't mind." She fluffed up the pillows and avoided those startling eyes, turning to get the tray. "Does your hand hurt?"

"I'd say no if I thought you'd believe me."

"The doctor left medicine." She picked up the bottle from the washstand.

Ben shook his head. "It makes me sleepy." He looked up at her ruefully. "I didn't mean for you to see the rest of the house yet."

She pulled a caned chair close to the bed and sat down. "I'm sorry. I didn't mean to invade your privacy, but I couldn't help it."

He shrugged a little. "It was supposed to be a surprise."

"What was?"

"The pictures. The garden. All of it."

"For who? For me?"

"Of course. Who else?" His eyes were innocent now, and the depth of his feeling leaped out at her.

"You did all of this ..." She looked at the garden wall. "... for me?"

"Yes. I was hoping one day you would see it. Under different circumstances, of course."

"It's beautiful." She looked slowly around, from the garden gate to the toad, to the butterflies and the ivy, not quite able or willing to follow his statement to its logical conclusion.

"So are you," he said softly.

"Ben ..." She knew her feelings for him had grown and blossomed like the garden, but she wasn't sure she was ready to confront them.

He smiled at her. "Marry me, Judith."

She lowered her lashes, unable to return his direct gaze. She wanted to say yes, but the thought itself frightened her a little, and she felt bound by her duties at home. "I can't right now."

"Why not?" His disappointment was palpable, and it made her ache.

"Father—"

"He doesn't hate me, does he?"

"No. But the children—"

"Your father will be home to stay in a month or two, and Joel is home," Ben reasoned. "They can exist without you, Judith. And you'll only be a few yards up the road. You can help your sisters out whenever they need you. Unless you'd prefer to live in town. I could get a job with the daily paper anytime. The editor's told me so."

She smiled, shaking her head.

"I will, if you want me to."

"I couldn't live in town," she said. "Besides, you'd have to paint another house then."

A fire kindled in his blue eyes. "Take this away." He pushed at the tray, so that the coffee slopped over the rim of the cup and soaked his napkin.

She held it firm. "No, you need to eat."

"Judith."

"You need to eat, Ben." She looked deep into his eyes and found she wasn't afraid anymore. She reached out and touched his cheek gently with her fingertips. "We'll talk about this when you're better."

*****

Ben stayed away from River Rest for the next two weeks, but Judith wasn't fretful about it. The joy and inner peace she had found the day of his injury stayed with her. She sent meals up to him by Joel and bleached the blood-stained towels. She managed to get the stains out of his fine cotton shirt, and sent it back crisply pressed. Joel brought her daily reports of Ben's progress, and she was content.

She was rolling pie crust in the middle of the morning, with her sleeves rolled up and her mother's big apron covering her blouse and skirt, when Joel and Ben walked into her kitchen.

"Well, hello," she said in surprise. Ben smiled at her almost shyly, and she felt a rush of anticipation. He was holding a small box, but said nothing, so Judith smiled back and turned to her brother.

Joel opened the dish cupboard. "Ben's out of coffee. Can we get a cup?"

"Of course." Judith preferred tea, but Joel had acquired a taste for coffee while working in the print shop, and she brewed it every morning now. She suspected he and Ben drank it by the gallon. She had pushed the coffee pot to the back of the range after breakfast. Joel brought two cups, and she poured them full, glad they had gotten a fresh supply of coffee beans that week. Ben and Joel carried their cups into the dining room.

"Join us, Judith," Joel called.

"In a minute." She crimped the crust around the edge of the last mince pie and placed it carefully in the oven, then made herself a cup of tea. Before leaving the kitchen, she washed her hands, took off the apron, unrolled her sleeves, and buttoned her cuffs.

"Where's Joel?" she asked at the dining room doorway. Ben sat alone at the table.

"He went upstairs for something."

Judith hesitated.

Ben's eyes were warm and eager. "Sit down, Judith. You promised me we'd talk when I was better. Well, I'm better."

"Is your hand well?"

"Pretty near. It will take a while for everything to finish knitting, but Ed thinks I'll use my fingers again. No infection. He's pretty happy with it." He held up his hand. The fingers were scarred and discolored, still a little swollen.

"I'm glad it's healing." She settled in one of the ladderback chairs and sipped her tea, her heart beating rapidly. "I haven't seen you much lately."

"I've been making the *Hummer* turn a profit and trying my hardest to get better."

She nodded.

Ben hesitated, then pushed the box he had brought an inch toward her on the tabletop. "I brought something for you."

She reached slowly for the box and removed the cover, unable to say anything. A sheet of paper lay on top of layers of cotton batting. She unfolded it slowly.

"Am I meant to read this?"

"If you like. It's from a friend of mine in New York. He was kind enough to take on a commission for me."

*Dear Ben,* she read, *The detailed drawing you sent leads me to believe the ornament was a delicate glass star, made by Wilfred Bryant, of Canterbury, England. Bryant made many such ornaments between 1820 and 1850, but only a few found their way to the States. It has taken me several months, but a dealer on Park Avenue located this one for me at last. It is similar to your design, but I am told no two were identical, so I hope it is near enough to satisfy you. Next time you are in the city ... Dan Hughes.*

Very slowly, Judith separated the layers of cotton. Winking at her from its soft resting place was a glass star, so like her mother's that she gasped. Its delicate beauty amazed her.

"Take it out," Ben urged quietly, watching her face.

"Oh, no, I couldn't. I'd be sure to drop it." She looked up at him quickly, her pulse racing. "This cost you a great deal."

"None of that. I'm just sorry it wasn't here in time for Christmas."

His eyes were as blue as the blue jay that screamed on the bird feeder outside the window. She couldn't stop looking into them, but she couldn't think of anything to say, either. *Serenity,* she counseled herself, trying to slow her pounding heart. *A quiet spirit.* There were many, many things she would like to say, but she couldn't think how to lead into them. Better to say nothing than to blunder into blurting out something she would regret.

Ben saved her the trouble.

"Judith, I have told you that I love you. I want to marry you. Please, can we talk about it now?"

She tried to lift her cup again, but her hand shook so that she set it down again. "All right. Let's talk."

"Joel and I are pretty close."

"That's good," she said cautiously.

"Yes, well, he may have unintentionally misled me for a while there as to how you felt about me."

"I think you're right," she said softly. "I'm sorry, Ben."

"I shouldn't have listened to him. But there's one thing. He tells me you have some questions. Is he right about that?"

She looked down at her teacup. "You don't need to tell me anything, Ben."

"I want to." He leaned toward her. "I want things to be plain and open between us."

Judith swallowed. "Well, I *have* wondered."

"About the past?"

"Yes. And what drove you here."

He looked away and breathed deeply, then faced her.

"I've only been in love once before, Judith."

She waited for him to go on, not sure she wanted to hear what he would say.

"Her name was ... Helen. My boss's daughter. We were married two years. Not very long." He picked up his spoon and stared at it as if it were priceless silver. "She died in childbirth. The baby, too. It was ... not the best moment of my life."

Judith felt tears in her eyes. "Ben, I'm sorry. I shouldn't have asked."

"Yes, you should." He laid the spoon down. "You have to know. You can't just marry someone without knowing these things. She ... she was very different from you. Not as spirited. And she wasn't strong, from the start. It was a very difficult time for me. Her family was kind to me, but I couldn't stand to stay there, with all the reminders. So I left." He smiled sadly. "That's it. I mean, unless you want to know more about it."

"No. It's enough. Maybe someday, when we're eating breakfast in the kitchen with the birds, you'll tell me more. But it's enough for now."

He looked at her steadily, then nodded. "Anything else, then? I'll tell you anything."

"I don't know where to start," she confessed.

"I'm thirty-three years old, I have eight thousand dollars in the bank, and I'm planning to expand the print shop, build onto the house. We can have the dining room back then."

She laughed. "Will you paint in there for me?"

"Anything you want. And I'll throw in a table and chairs of your choosing." He reached over and took her hand. "Not still scared of me, are you?"

She shook her head.

"Will you marry me, Judith?"

"Yes," she said softly, a deep joy shooting through her.

He nodded, smiling. "When?"

She smiled slowly. "How long will it take you to finish painting the garden in the bedroom?"

He considered. "I could stay up all night tonight and do it."

She laughed.

"I thought I'd put an elderberry bush beside the door, and maybe a swing on the north wall. What do you want in your garden?"

"It's already more wonderful than anything I could have imagined. I think your ideas are much more beautiful than mine."

"All right, I'll paint whatever strikes me." Ben stood up and held out his hand to her. Judith stood, and he drew her into his arms. "You'll need to get word to your Father. Is two weeks all right?"

She gulped. "Yes."

"You sure? Because I can wait a bit longer."

She looked up at him and knew she wanted what he wanted, and she didn't want to set him a distant goal. "If you don't mind a simple ceremony," she whispered, lowering her eyelids. There wouldn't be time to sew a gown. She would have to consult her aunts. Perhaps there was something in the family she could borrow. If not, she would wear her Sunday dress and be happy.

Ben looked extremely satisfied. "Simple is good."

"Will your family be upset if you marry so suddenly?" she asked.

"I don't think so. They'll be thrilled. Perhaps we could drive out there next fall and visit. Do you think it's possible?"

Her head was whirling with thoughts of the future, near and distant.

"I'd like to meet your family sometime."

"Good." His smile was irrepressible. "I guess I've got my work cut out for me for the next few days. You'll have your wall garden for the rest of the winter, and if you get tired of it, I'll paint over it next summer and give you a jungle or a circus or something."

"I don't think I'll ever get tired of it, Ben."

He bent his head to kiss her, his eyes gleaming, and Judith let her hands glide slowly up onto his shoulders. He was so warm, so solid. When his lips touched hers, a shock of gladness rocked her. He released her just long enough for her to catch her breath, then kissed her again. It was odd, she thought fleetingly, how one could be so agitated, and yet so at peace. With delicious trepidation, she slid one hand up into his hair, and his hold on her tightened.

"Say, Ben—"

They both jumped as Joel stopped in the doorway.

Ben turned around and looked at him, gently pulling Judith's head down to rest peacefully against his shoulder.

"Sorry," Joel said sheepishly. "More news for the *Hummer*, I take it?"

THE END

Dear reader,

Thank you for reading River Rest. This book was partly inspired by my great-aunt Belle Goff's diary. Many of the events described in this story really happened, but most of them at a later date. Belle married a farmer who also ran a small newspaper and printed items like bills and butter paper. His name was Harry Thayer. Aunt Belle also enjoyed her bird feeder. She never had children of her own, but loved to spend time with her nieces and nephews. Her mother's maiden name was Chadbourne, which is why I chose that for the family in my story.

A few of the other events are rooted in truth. The Sidney Grange Hall really did burn down (but on a different date). Uncle Harry did injure his hand when he shut it in the printing press. He was quite an artist, and I have a few of his doodles that survived in letters to a family member and as holiday cards for relatives.

On the other side of the family, my Page grandparents loved theatricals and performed often in community productions. In 1896, a dozen family members, along with a few friends, produced the play *My Awful Dad*, mentioned in this story, followed by "the laughable farce, *Turn Him Out!*" They performed it at the Masonic Hall in Belgrade, Maine, across the lake from Sidney, where Belle's family lived. Belle's sister Emma later taught school in Belgrade and married Oral Page. She became my grandmother. Belle also taught school in the area. Sadly, Aunt Belle died from complications of appendicitis in 1939, and her journal ends abruptly.

This is not her story; it is fiction. The people in this book are fictional characters. But Judith's life parallel's Aunt Belle's in many ways. Belle's diary spans 1923 to 1939, and this story is set in 1918. The events borrowed from her diary are retold, not as fact, but as a basis for a story. I will always be thankful that she left us her diary, giving us such a vivid picture of farm life in Central Maine in the early 20<sup>th</sup> Century.

Thank you for reading my book!

Susan

Discussion Questions for River Rest

1. Why is Judith so concerned about people outside the family learning the Chadbournes' doings? How has this attitude changed in the last 100 years?

2. What else do you think Judith could have done to help her father near the beginning of the story?

3. Have you ever felt overwhelmed by your work and family concerns? How did you learn to cope?

4. Do you think Judith should have accepted Ben's offer to work for the newspaper?

5. In what ways is Christina trying to show her independence?

6. Joel and Ben think Judith is a bit prudish, overly concerned about what other people will think. Do you think she was overprotective of Christina? If not, why not?

7. What does each of these items mean to Judith: The bird feeder? Her father's gun? The treetop star? The quilt?

8. At what point does Judith show that she truly trusts Ben?

9. How do Judith's extended family help her? Should she have relied on them more?

10. Do you think Judith has an accurate picture of her mother's peace? How does her search for it come full circle?

**About the author**: Susan Page Davis is the author of more than sixty published novels. She's a two-time winner of the Inspirational Readers' Choice Award, and also a winner of the Carol Award and the Will Rogers Medallion, and a finalist in the WILLA Awards and the More Than Magic Contest. A Maine native, she now lives in Kentucky. Visit her website at: www.susanpagedavis.com , where you can sign up for her occasional newsletter, contact Susan, and read a short story on her romance page. If you liked this book, please consider writing a review and posting it on Amazon, Goodreads, or the venue of your choice.


READ MORE OF SUSAN PAGE DAVIS'S BOOKS:

More of Susan Page Davis's historical novels you might enjoy:

The Crimson Cipher (set in 1915)

The Outlaw Takes a Bride

The Seafaring Women of the Vera B. (Co-authored with Susan's son James S. Davis)

The Ladies' Shooting Club Series

    The Sheriff's Surrender

    The Gunsmith's Gallantry

    The Blacksmith's Bravery

Captive Trail

Cowgirl Trail

Heart of a Cowboy

The Prairie Dreams series

    The Lady's Maid

    Lady Anne's Quest

    A Lady in the Making

Maine Brides

White Mountain Brides

Wyoming Brides

Love Finds You in Prince Edward Island

Mystery and Suspense books by Susan Page Davis:
The Frasier Island Series:
    Frasier Island
    Finding Marie
    Inside Story
Just Cause
Witness
On a Killer's Trail
Hearts in the Crosshairs
What a Picture's Worth
The Mainely Mysteries Series (coauthored by Susan's daughter, Megan Elaine Davis)
    Homicide at Blue Heron Lake
    Treasure at Blue Heron Lake
    Impostors at Blue Heron Lake
Trail to Justice
And many more
    **See all of her books** at www.susanpagedavis.com and sign up for Susan's occasional newsletter.

CPSIA information can be obtained at www.ICGtesting.com
Printed in the USA
LVOW11s1918130916

504435LV00009B/905/P

9 780997 230833